A Fatal
Addiction

ISBN. 978-1-9164910-2-1

A Fatal Addiction

Part 1
THE SEDUCTION OF SPEED

By

Max. M. Power

Brooklands Members Banking … where the
Ghosts walk.

Introduction:
The Birth and Early Development of Motor Sport

Until 1895, every motorist had to follow a walking
man who would wave a red flag to warn the
population that a mechanical monster was
approaching.
The repeal of the Red Flag Act in 1896 paved the way
for speed to become the 20th century addiction. The
sound, smell and the sensation of it would drive and
define the lives of a certain type of man and woman
regardless of their perceived class or with
determination, even wealth.
In 1895 the first organised motor race was held in
France over public roads between Paris and Bordeaux,
it was won by Emile Levassor with his Panhard-
Levassor driven at a top speed of 18.5mph. These
early French races were all run on public roads and by
the turn of the century top speeds of more than
50mph had been reached. Thousands of people would
gather to watch these roaring, smoking machines
thunder past, usually in clouds of smoke and eye
stinging dust.
By 1903 speeds had increased and were now reaching
almost 100mph. The cars had become too fast for the
open public roads. Very poor road surface conditions,
animals and people wandering onto the narrow roads
and lack of visibility in the dust storms which
followed each cars progress made it "Russian roulette
at 90mph" as one contemporary driver described it.
The almost inevitable disaster happened in the Paris
to Madrid race before the cars had even reached half
way.

Two drivers, a mechanic and five spectators were killed in crashes. The race was stopped and racing on open public roads came to an immediate end.

In England, no "racing," would be allowed by law for another two years, but to celebrate the repeal of the red flag act, the Motor Car Club organized a run between London and Brighton. This event still carries on to this day.

The first car race on British soil, the Tourist Trophy in 1905 was held on The Isle of Man. This race attracted 42 starters and was won by J Napier driving an Arrol-Johnson averaging 33.9mph. The Isle of Man had been chosen as everywhere else in Great Britain a twenty mile an hour speed limit was imposed, and roads could not be closed, whereas the Manx Government could close roads whenever they wanted. With the building of the 3.75-mile Brooklands track by Hugh Locke-King in 1907, which became known as "The Birth Place of British Motor Racing", Britain had its first permanent motor racing circuit. It gave drivers and public their first opportunity to watch cars driven at speed without having to travel overseas for the experience

With typical English eccentricity, Brooklands was organized using many rules and ideas from the horse racing world. In fact, the first meeting held on 6th July 1907 was heralded as "a motor Ascot".

Until 1914 the drivers wore colored jackets rather than having numbers on their cars, bookmakers were allowed at Brooklands and cars handicapped as in horse racing. Entry prices for the public enclosures were set high to ensure the Brooklands motto of "the right crowd and no crowding" would prevail throughout the track's existence.

The development of motorcycles gave the less affluent a chance to experience the thrill of speed. Many young men began their speed addiction in this way, and through their start in motorcycle racing, the best became very successful and famous racing drivers.

In 1907as the great concrete bowl of Brooklands was being created from marsh and woodland in Surrey, the Isle of Man was chosen to host the first major motorcycle race in a Great Britain. For the first four years a "short" course was used as early motorcycles were mainly single gear, belt-drive models which could not climb the mountain section of the course. Since 1911 the narrow 37-mile course has remained largely unchanged to his day. The TT races are still considered to be the most challenging and dangerous motor cycle races in the world.

In Europe racing developed much quicker than in England, using closed public roads, and it gave Italy and France the opportunity to become the leading manufacturers of racing cars. In 1906 France organised the first Grand Prix which was held at Le Mans. Not on the circuit to be made famous in the 1920s, but using a 64-mile lap on the lanes and dusty roads around the city. The race was won by Hungarian driver Ferenc Szisz driving a cherry red 12.9 litre Renault averaging 62.9mph. Renault had fitted the new development of Michelin detachable rims, which gave them considerable advantage. The poor condition of the roads caused many punctures, the scourge of these early races.

Szisz is a good example of the opportunities the birth of motor sport offered young men at the turn of the century. An engineer in Hungary he moved to Paris and joined Renault in 1900. He became riding mechanic for Marcel Renault, but when Marcel was killed in the 1903 Paris-Madrid race Louis Renault promoted Szisz to driver. With his win in the 1906 race he became a Hungarian hero.

Also, in 1906, held for the first time in Italy, was the famous road race the Targa Florio around the bandit-ridden Sicilian roads. The initial race was run over three laps of the islands coastal, a 92.47-mile circuit. It was won by Alessandro Cagno driving an Itala.

Cagno, like Szisz, came from a working-class background. He became an apprentice engineer and his passion for mechanics saw him become the third employee of FIAT. He also started as a riding mechanic, taking part in the ill-fated Paris-Madrid race. His driving ability saw Cagno promoted to racing driver and in 1906 he joined another famous Turin manufacturer Itala for whom he won many races including at first Targa Florio.

The skill and daring of these flamboyant characters produced the first super stars of motor racing one of the best being Felice Nazzaro the son of a Turin coal merchant. Nazzaro was said to "handle a car like a violin". One of his greatest young fans was Enzo Ferrari.

The Peugeot Grand Prix cars of 1912 were to revolutionize engine development with their overhead valves and twin overhead camshafts. They won the 1912 French Grand Prix and set the general layout for all future racing engines.

The year1914 would bring the end of motor sport for several years, but even before the war had started

Mercedes had already invaded France. They sent five of their 4.5litre four-cylinder cars, producing 110bhp, to the French Grand Prix. The race brought heartbreak for French hero Georges Boillot who while leading in his 4.4 litre Peugeot retired on the last lap. This heart-breaking retirement allowed Mercedes to take the first three places. It was to be an uncomfortable omen of thing to come.

After the war advances in mechanical development were rapid. The war had brought significant improvements in designs and metallurgy. By 1920 many new exciting cars were appearing from manufacturers like Ballot, Peugeot, Sunbeam, and from America, Duesenberg and Miller.
Duesenberg entered four of their sleek white and blue cars for the 1921 French Grand Prix held at Le Mans. Much to the shock of the European manufactures, after a tremendous dual with a Ballot driven by another American de Palma, they won the race with Jimmy Murphy driving.
These Duesenberg cars were the first to use hydraulic brakes, a system designed by Scots born Malcolm Loughead, who later spelt his name Lockheed. This name is now synonymous with vehicle braking systems.
Racing at Brooklands re-started in 1920. It was still the main outlet for motor sport in England and the most important for vehicle and engine development. The racing was diverse. A handicapping system allowed cars of all sizes and power to compete from little Austin 7's to Aero engine monsters.
Record breaking attempts were constant and increasing numbers of specialist magnificent aero machines were built to raise the speeds ever higher.

The all-time outright circuit lap record was set by John Cobb driving the magnificent 24 litre Napier-Railton at 143.43mph.

Racing at Brooklands finally ended with the outbreak of the Second World War. Too much damage had been done in the war to make repairs viable when hostilities ended.

In 1923 a race was first held which would arguably become the most famous race in the world, The Le Mans 24 Hours. Winning this race soon became an obsession for motor manufactures and drivers from France, Italy, Germany, England, and America.

The British have always had a love affair with Le Mans and in 1924 the Bentley 3litre of Duff and Clement won the race.

Bentley has won the race four more times, so far. Each year many thousands of British fans make the pilgrimage to Le Mans. The race has helped to make names like Ferrari, Jaguar, Porsche and more recently Audi world famous.

The Isle of Man TT races have always been regarded as the prestigious and oldest motorcycle race. It has proved to be the most dangerous motorcycle road-race in the world.

The obsession for motorcycle manufactures and riders was, from the very early years, and still is today, winning a Hermes Statue Silver Trophy in a TT race on the Isle of Man. For more than a week each June the island is invaded by bikers from all over the world wanting to experience this unique event.

Two other race circuits feature in the story that follows. Both have also played a major part in the development of motor sport development before the Second World War.

Spa Francorchamps, situated in the Forests' of the Ardennes in South Eastern Belgium, has long been considered the most challenging and dangerous track in the world. The unpredictable climate of the area can result in parts of the circuit being dry while unseen around the next 120mph turn the track is soaking wet.

First used in 1922 it was formed on a roughly triangle shape with ultra-fast bends and no margin for error It has always filled drivers with terror and acute pleasure in equal measure.

In 1939 the track was altered with the removal of the Virage de I'Ancienne Douanne corner, to give the racing driver one of the most daunting challenges in the world, the addition of Eau Rouge corner.

In 1931 the first purpose-built road circuit in England was opened at Donington Park in Derbyshire. The first car race meeting was held on 25th March 1933, and it soon became an important place for racing motorcycles and cars.

Donington Park went on to host the Donington Grand Prix's of the late 1930s which for two years featured the sensational German "Silver Arrows" cars. Adolf Hitler was reported to have given the German mark equivalent of a twenty-thousand-pound grant to Mercedes to develop a new racing car "for the honor of Germany"

(This would be the equivalent of over one million UK pounds today). Hitler also invested thousands of marks in Mercedes German rivals Auto Union. In 1934 the sensational Mercedes W25 raced and won for the first time. Mercedes won four major races and

Auto Union three in 1934. For the following five
years the Germans dominated Grand Prix racing.
These Silver Arrows "invaded" England twice in 1937
and 1938

Auto Union cars won both races at Donington Park
with

Bernard Rosemeyer victorious the first year and when
Rosemeyer was tragically killed trying to break speed
records Tazio Nuvolari became the star team driver,
winning in 1938.

These famous race circuits all play important parts in
the following story,

A Fatal Addiction, which charts the fortunes of two
families and the impact motor sport passion, had on
their lives.

Dedicated to the memory of all those riders and

Drivers', who have paid the ultimate price

in their pursuit of speed.

1

"Push, Push, Push! Please, my dear, just one more time," anxious midwife Agnes Willes pleaded to Mary Cartland. It had been eight hours since Mary's labour had started. Now darkness crept through the small bedroom in Forge Cottage where she lay.

Now completely exhausted, Mary had been in pain and pushing for hours.

With one final piercing cry, signaling a final effort, Mary pushed again, and at last a bloodied baby boy was born.

There followed silence. No sound from mother or baby.

Mary Cartland had suffered a devastating heart attack.

Agnes gently picked up the child and pressed him between her large, soft breasts. Her sobs began slowly, the tears gently running down her cheeks, but soon she was gulping at air and the sobs became a wail.

A muffled, whine-like noise came from the sticky red mess between her breasts. She glanced down at the baby who opened one eye and screamed. Agnes looked at the now peaceful face of Mary and then again at the angry, red-faced tiny boy she was holding. Tears flowed freely down Agnes' cheeks as she whispered,

"What a terrible waste. I'm afraid he will soon be joining you, my dearest girl. I can't imagine this little mite lasting more than a week."

Agnes Willes had delivered babies in Burlham for more than 30 years; including Mary's four other children.

Mary Cartland had been her only daughter.

Agnes carried the screaming, tiny bundle out of the small bedroom to the rest of his family, who were silently siting around the kitchen table… waiting.

"You have another son, Charlie," she said to the giant of a man now standing in front of her... "Would you like to hold him?"
Pushing past her, Charlie snarled,
"Keep that screaming brat quiet, I want my Mary."
Charlie went into the bedroom and for twenty long seconds the family in the kitchen heard no noise. Then a mighty, almost inhuman howl came from the bedroom.
Agnes rushed the baby out of the house, afraid of what Charlie would do the next time he saw him.
For a long-time the four Cartland children waited nervously in the kitchen, unsure of how to react. Suddenly their father burst out of the bedroom, walked past them all and, slamming the door behind him, left the house without saying a word.
Charlie Cartland was drunk for two days but did manage to sober up on the third day for his wife's burial.

The baby, born on the 28th July 1899, named Frank by his sister Joan, was a fighter and proved his grandmother wrong. Agnes had found a wet nurse in the next village who was happy to feed the baby, and she managed to keep him safe from his father. Agnes cared for Frank, with help from his eldest sister Joan, in her own small cottage for the first 12 months of his life.

After his first birthday Frank was returned to his home where he continued to thrive, growing into a healthy boy, raised by sisters Joan and Edith. During those early years Frank was generally ignored by his father Charlie, and by his two elder brothers, John and Joe.

From the beginning of the nineteenth Century, the Cartland family had been blacksmiths in the village of Burlham, A small village standing on the chalk marl slope at the edge of the Fens in Cambridgeshire.

At the turn of the twentieth century, village life revolved around the three pubs and the imposing village church of St Mary's.

St Mary's had been rebuilt 100 years previously, after lightning had destroyed its tower. A church had stood on the site for more than 800 years and it was easy to see why. Constructed on the only high ground in the village, the grand building looked out over the Fens towards Ely Cathedral, ten miles distant.

It also looked down with a seemingly aloof air on the village and its Burlham congregation.

Two hundred yards down the lane, past the Red Lion pub, stood the Blacksmith's Forge. The Blacksmith's Forge was a place of contrasts.

During the day it was hot, bright and full of sharp, loud noise, with the pungent mixed smells of horse sweat and smoke. When darkness descended it became a sinister place: silent, grimy, full of dark shadows, with the hint of movement in corners just out of sight. There was one small, high window that let in the only natural daylight.

Behind the forge a cobbled yard led to a small, four-roomed cottage. The kitchen and living area made up the main room of Forge cottage. The kitchen space contained a big, square, stained pine table at its centre, and a large, old black cooking range, which provided the only heating in the cottage.

The smell of a hundred years of accumulated smoke permeated through the walls and furniture, while the low ceilings gave the cottage a claustrophobic feel.

Frank slept on a small and narrow horsehair bed in the corner of a room shared with his two brothers. His two sisters shared another room, while their father Charlie had the smallest room for himself. Once a week the family took turns for their weekly wash in an old tin tub placed in front of the kitchen range. The water heated on the range had to be drawn from the well in the back garden. From the well, a gravel path descended to a brick shed at the bottom of the garden, which housed the earth closet. From the age of seven, when he was big enough to lift the bucket, emptying it when necessary became Frank's job. This was a job that Joe had been more than happy to pass on to his younger brother.

"I've had the shit job long enough, now it's your turn," Joe had said with a grin. "It's my birthday present to you." Being the youngest of the five children, Frank accepted the job without protest.

There were good reasons for his compliance. In recent years their father Charlie had become even more sullen and short-tempered. He ran the household by fear, drank heavily and continued to blame Frank for his Mary's death. Without Mary's controlling influence, Charlie felt lost and impotent. All the villagers in Burlham knew Charlie Cartland had a violent temper. Nicknamed "Iron Hand", he had been the most feared fast bowler in the county of Cambridgeshire. That was until he was banned from playing cricket.

The nickname came from Charlie spending years working the blacksmith forge, where small slivers of molten metal would fly off the, orange hot, iron he would hammer and shape into horseshoes and all forms of farm and household implements.

Some slivers would land on Charlie and burn their way unnoticed into his hand and forearm. Over the years some slivers became permanently embedded in his flesh. Being 6ft tall and weighing 15st, he had the strength of an ox. Charlie struck a trembling fear into all the batsmen that had to face his bowling.

Seeing this black-haired, bearded giant rushing towards them with a very hard ball in his hand, the metal implants glinting in the sun, was enough to make even the bravest quake in their cricket boots.

The cricket ban came in September 1906. Burlham playing in the final of the Cambs Cup against their bitter rivals, the village of Moreton. It had been a very close match and Burlham needed just two wickets for victory. When the team captain gave the ball to Charlie for his final over, success looked almost certain. Charlie rushed in to bowl and the red ball thundered hard into the pads of the Moreton batsman.

"Howzat!" roared Charlie. Usually whenever Charlie appealed for leg before wicket (LBW), his roar and intimidating stare made it certain the umpire would raise his finger. But this brave soul said:

"Not out".

"What do you mean? That was fucking out!" screamed Charlie into the poor man's face.

"It was not out," repeated the trembling umpire, as beads of sweat formed on his forehead. A quick left hook from Charlie and the umpire was out himself...with a broken jaw. Charlie never played cricket again.

For the slightest reason, Charlie would take his belt to Frank, usually when he'd come home from the pub drunk. The other children were too afraid to try and stop him. The latest trigger for violence came on a cold November night. Frank was ten years old.
He had forgotten to call after school on the local farmer, Albert Betts. He was meant to pick up the three pounds owed to Charlie for shoeing one of the farmer's Shire horses. It had been very late when Frank arrived home.
"Where's the money, Frank?" said his worried sister Joan, the moment her brother entered the cottage. "Father will be home soon, and he'll be expecting it."
Frank had been very happy until that moment. Now fear cramped his belly.
"I … I was going to pick it up, but I forgot, he explained nervously. "There's a new steam engine working in the Fens, and I went to see that instead."

By pub closing time, the tension in the cottage was palpable.
"Where's that useless little runt? He was supposed to bring my money to the pub," raged a very angry and drunk Charlie Cartland as he staggered into the cottage. He was waving the strap he used on his youngest son in his right hand. From his hiding place in the corner of the kitchen, behind his sisters, Frank could see the strap hanging from the large iron fist. It was big, wide and worn, and Frank knew it hurt like hell.
"Come out from there you little piece of shit," shouted Charlie when he saw him. Grabbing a handful of

6

his hair he dragged Frank out from behind his sisters' skirts. The other children sat still and watched silently. Out in the yard, Charlie threw Frank down hard onto the sharp flint cobbles. Giving him a firm kick he shouted,

"I wish you had never been fucking born, you should have died, not my Mary."

There was a loud, sharp crack as he brought the strap down hard on Frank's back and thighs. Pain shot through him, and he desperately clung to the thought, I have to keep quiet, I have to keep quiet. After all the other beatings he'd suffered, he knew he must not call out. During the first few beatings, Frank had cried, "I'm sorry; I'm sorry, please stop hitting me." But that had enraged Charlie and he always hit him harder.

So now, his face pressed hard into the icy cobbles, Frank lay still, eyes tight shut, silently biting back the tears and the pain. To help, he escaped into his private dream world.

I am running fast through the field of ripe barley. My bare body is warmed by the hot sun. I'm lost, near the centre of the field, where the tops of the golden yellow stalks are higher than my head. Breathless, I stop and lie down. Swallowed by the barley, I look up into the cloudless, deep blue sky. Alone and happy I close my eyes. I can hear the buzzing bees and flies, noisy and busy, all around me. The barley ears whisper to me in the breeze, their fine hairs sway like the wispy strands of an old man's hair.

Suddenly Frank felt a sharp pain, pain like the worst toothache, and his ribs immediately felt the hard, cold cobbles again.

By the time Charlie had tried of the beating, Frank had lost count of the number of times he had been hit. Frank opened one eye and looked up to see Charlie clutching his stomach. He closed his eye again, just in time. Charlie retched and a stream of stinking, steaming sick spewed over Frank's face and hair. With a final hard kick into Frank's ribs, Charlie turned and staggered back to his bedroom. When Charlie had gone, Joan rushed out. She gently lifted Frank off the cobbles and carried him back into the cottage.

"That's the last time I'll let him do this to me," Frank said quietly as Joan gently cleaned the foul -smelling mess from his hair and face. "I promise you I'll kill him first."

"Don't talk like that, Frank. You know he doesn't mean it, it's just the drink what does it. He didn't drink so much before mother died."
As Joan held a cold, wet cloth to the large red welts growing on Frank's thin, white thighs, she added: "You will just have to try not to upset him so much."
Frank's back, thighs and ribs hurt, but his head was clear. He was sure he would carry out his threat to kill his father one day. Even at ten years old he knew he would need to be patient and probably have to take more beatings before he was strong enough to carry out his promise. In the meantime, he would just try to keep out of his father's way.

Every Sunday morning the whole Cartland family would put on their best clothes and make the short walk up the hill to St Mary's church. Frank hated Sundays. He always found it very uncomfortable wearing a shirt, tie and his best short trousers.
The family pew of dark oak was situated in the third row from the back, on the right-hand side of the aisle. The pew was black with age and very hard; it felt to Frank as if he was sitting on a lump of old iron.

It was always especially painful if the Sunday came soon after a beating from his father. The old church was forever cold, with icy drafts curling around his bare legs, giving him goose pimples. The endless droning sermons of the vicar, Reverend Walter Sexton, always made him feel very unhappy.

"If there is a God why did he let our mother die?" he had asked the vicar after one service.

"It is not our place to question God's actions, young man," replied Walter Sexton, obviously irritated by being spoken to by a ten-year-old boy. "Your mother is in a much better place than here on this earth. She's at God's side." Before Frank could reply, Joan had pulled him away.

"I don't believe him, and I don't believe in God," Frank said quietly to Joan as they walked back through the churchyard. Past his mother's grave in the Cartland family plot and made their way to Forge Cottage.
On the Sunday after Frank's latest beating, Joan had been surprised to see him kneeling in the pew, with eyes screwed up, silently mouthing a prayer, although she was fearful of what he was praying for.

In fact, Frank didn't have to carry out the promise he had made to Joan. Just one month after that last heavy beating, at 6am on a freezing Monday morning in December, Frank made his way across the moonlit, frost capped cobbles of the icy yard. His morning duty was to light the fire pit in the forge. He had to make sure there was a good working fire when Charlie was ready to start work. He knew a fresh beating was almost certain if the fire was not hot enough. Straining to push open the heavy oak door, the smell hit Frank. Mixed with the expected smoky, horsey stench of the forge he was accustomed to, was the distinctive smell of their outhouse - the smell of shit and piss. In the dim, early morning light shining through the small forge window, he could just make out, hanging from the massive black beam that ran the length of the forge, the body of his father. Frank's first reaction was to turn and run, but instead he was drawn slowly towards the gently swaying body hanging next to the massive forge anvil. Curious, he stood looking up at the staring eyes of the vast shell that had been his father, not with any sadness, just with a growing sense of relief.

 A shout of "Frank!" cause him to turn. A black silhouette in the forge doorway was his sister Joan.

"Get away from there!" she screamed. Rushing in, she grabbed his arm and dragged him back to the cottage. Seeing his distressed sister and brother burst into the cottage, John ran into the forge.

He soon returned to the shocked family, who were huddled together in front of the range.

"Looks like the old man is dead," he said bluntly, breaking the shocked silence.

"Joe, run off and fetch Constable Clarke and then cycle over to get Doctor Jones." said Joan.

Joe set off and the others waited, without a word, until Joe and Constable Tom Clarke returned twenty minutes later. Constable Clarke, with John alongside, went into the forge. Together they managed to cut Charlie down. Later that morning Doctor Jones arrived. After ten minutes he walked into the cottage and announced to the children,

"I'm sorry to have to confirm that your father has died. He appears to have hanged himself."

Doctor Jones wasn't surprised that there were no tears. His news was met by silence from the five children in the cottage.

Charlie Cartland, aged 51, was buried next to his beloved wife Mary in the churchyard of St Mary's, up the hill from the forge.

The funeral was a very small affair, just the children and a few of Charlie's drinking and old cricketing mates attended. In total, ten people huddled around the grave. They stood in cold, driving sleet as the Reverend Sexton muttered the few, standard words:

"We now commit his body to the ground. Earth to earth ..." At that moment, with the sharp sound of dry dirt hitting the wooden lid of his father's coffin, Frank smiled with the sudden realisation that his nightmare was over. Walking slowly back down the path from the churchyard, the small party were all silent, heads down against the icy wind as the sleet turned to wet snow.

Christmas 1909 should have been the happiest that the Cartland children had experienced since their mother died. Two days before the big day, Joan and Edith were making plum Christmas pudding, their mood in the cottage relaxed and happy. The air, for once, smelled sweet, as the tang of oranges and brandy invaded the room. Joe and Frank were helping the girls.

"Stop eating the candied peel and nuts you two," scolded Joan. Then, turning to Frank, she said:

"Make yourself useful and run to the butchers to pick up the turkey we have ordered."

Just as Frank was about to leave, John arrived at the cottage, followed by a serious-looking Constable Tom Clarke and two other policemen.

"I'm sorry, Joan, but we need to ask you all some questions about Charlie," said Tom Clarke. "This is Inspector Davies from Cambridge Police Headquarters." Inspector Davies stepped forward. He was a small, nervous-looking man with a pencil-black moustache and straight, slicked-back black hair.

"Do any of you know what your father's movements were on the night before he died?" he said bluntly in a surprisingly-deep voice. His question was directed at Joan, as she was the eldest.

"As far as we know he went to the pub as usual then I heard him come in around eleven o'clock," she answered.

"Why are you asking? You know he killed himself."

"Yes, of course we know that," Inspector Davies replied with a, sharp, superior air. "But we have found a body, and it's someone your father used to visit".

"Whose body is it?" said Joan; her voice had also become sharp and high-pitched. She didn't like the tone of this horrid little man. The other four children remained silent.

"I can't tell you that just that it's a woman's body, and it's someone known to have given sexual favours to your father."

There followed a full minute of shocked silence. John was looking very pale and shaking slightly as he spoke for the first time.

"Where'd you find her?" he asked quietly.

Turning to look up at him, Inspector Davies said,

"My, my, you're a big lad, you must be John. Constable Clarke has told me about you."

Tom Clarke looked nervous as John gave him a long, hard stare.

"As I told your sister, I can't tell you any more at present, but the victim did put up a hell of a struggle. That's why we need to dig up your father's body, to see if it shows any signs of a fight."

"No," screamed Joan, as she leapt up and beat her fists into the chest of the inspector, almost knocking the surprised little man over. "Leave him in peace, he was always getting into fights, doesn't mean he killed anyone." John and Edith gently pulled Joan away and eased her onto a chair at the kitchen table. Flustered, the inspector said sharply,

"I'm sorry, but it has to be done." Without another word he turned and walked out of the cottage.

After the police had gone, Frank asked Joe:

"What are sexual favours?"

"You will find out soon enough, when you're older," was all Joe would say.

Frank was confused. He knew John had also been out that night and he had heard him arrive home around the same time as their father. He wondered why John hadn't told the inspector this.

None of the children were able to get much sleep. Frank lay in his narrow bed staring into the blackness and listening to the sobs of his sisters in the next room. Very early the next morning, Christmas Eve, the police dug up the body of Charlie Cartland, despite his family's protests. They took the body to Addenbrooks Hospital in Cambridge for the postmortem.

"They won't find anything. He couldn't have killed anybody," said Joan to no one in particular, as she, Joe, Edith and Frank sat around the kitchen table at first light. John wasn't at home. He had gone out to the pub the previous day, soon after the police left. By closing time, he had passed out on the floor of the Red Lion. Leaving him there, the landlord had locked up and gone to bed. Staggering back in the early hours, John had gone straight into the forge. Edith sat quietly sobbing as she always did when upset. Joe and Frank were silent and sullen as they listened to the dull, constant hammering coming from the forge. With a big sigh Frank said,

"We will never be free of our old man. Even when he's dead he still brings us misery."

No one answered him.

A cold but dry Christmas morning arrived. There had been no contact with the Cartland family from the police. At Joan's instance, they all went to St Mary's church for the 10am Christmas service. The family held their heads high in a real show of unity as they walked to the church. For once Frank was happy to put on his Sunday best.

None of the family had spoken about the police visit.

The previous night the local gravedigger, Walter Williams, had, for the price of a few pints, let the locals at the Red Lion know that he had spent the early hours of that morning digging up Charlie Cartland's coffin. The news and speculation had spread around the village like wildfire. The church congregation stopped their murmuring and gossip as the Cartland family filed into their black pew.

Revered Sexton had made the theme of his sermon sins of the flesh. His words had no meaning for Frank, so as usual when unhappy his mind went to a better place.

It is early on a warm spring day. A ground mist rises slowly from the ditch, as if from a wet grass fire. I'm sitting on the bank at the top of the Devil's Ditch, watching the rising mist and the rabbits. There are hundreds of the little furry brown bundles digging out the holes to their burrows. Their efforts are leaving a white chalk tear on the green slope as they busily continue their excavations. Chalkhill Blue butterflies have settled on the grass stems next to me, opening their wings to catch the warming morning sun. What's that? I can see something glinting in the weak sun at the bottom of the ditch; I'm sliding down the bank to investigate. Here amongst the white chalk rubble there's a golden, jeweled dagger. I'm bending down to pick it up.

Joe dug his elbow into Frank's ribs, and the dagger had gone.

"Come on; wake up Frank," he whispered. "The service has finished." Filing out of the church, many of their friends in the congregation avoided the Cartlands. They weren't prepared to speak to them, not even to wish them a happy Christmas.

"It's like they think they might catch something horrible from us," said a sobbing Joan as the group walked slowly home.

John usually spent his days alone now, and even on Christmas Day he immediately stripped off his suit after church, put on his overalls and went straight to the forge. The other children could hear the sharp sound of his heavy hammer striking the anvil, and the sudden hiss from the red-hot metal as he plunged a new horseshoe into the water trough.

All afternoon Joan, Edith, Joe and Frank sat quietly around the old pine table, their Christmas dinner cold and barely touched in front of them.

No one was in the mood for food or any of the usual party games, which Frank had always looked forward to in previous years.

By 4pm the darkness was creeping across the room like a black, grasping shadow. Joe got up and walked slowly through each room of the silent cottage, lighting the oil lamps to banish the cold dark night from their home.

The cause of the Cartland family's distress had been found in the river by Billy Webb and Eric Foulds, who were both ten years old and lived in the village of Farewell. Billy's dad was the local milkman, so Billy was always up early. Two days before Christmas he went around to Eric's house and threw some stones on his window to wake him up.

They arrived at the Lode in Farewell early, around 6.30am, intending to do some illegal pike fishing. This was something Farewell boys had done for generations.

The pike in Farewell Lode could grow to more than thirty pounds. It was the ambition, probably the only ambition, of many of the young lads in the area to catch one of these monster fish. Billy was using live bait, a small roach that he had just caught. They had been casting for half an hour without success when he felt a tug on his line and made a hard strike. In an excited voice he shouted across to Eric,

"Get the gaff ready, I've got a bloody whopper here."
He pulled hard, his fishing rod bending almost double and in danger of breaking.

"Come on, help me with it, I've never felt anything as big as this before," he shouted to Eric. They were expecting a long hard struggle to land a huge pike. Together they slowly started to reel in Billy's catch, surprised and a little disappointed that it was not putting up much of a fight.

"Here it comes," shouted Eric as a light shape began to appear towards the surface.

The first thing they saw was a foot. Then a leg up to the thigh rose out of the water, like a surfacing submarine. They could clearly see Billy's three-barbed hook embedded deep into the stark white flesh. The remains of the roach were still on the hook and appeared to be nibbling at the leg.

The boy's nerve went at that moment. They dropped the fishing rod, and ran to the closest building. This was the Anglers Arms Pub. Crying and distressed, they hammered on the door until the landlord finally opened it.

"What the hell..." he started to say, angry at being disturbed so early.

"There ... there's a body in the water," stammered Billy. Both boys were by now hysterical.

After they had managed to blurt out their tale, the landlord left them with his wife and rushed round to the police house. The landlord and constable returned to the riverbank, found Billy's fishing rod and, with difficulty, pulled the body from the water.

Later that morning, the doctor, Howard Jones, arrived. He quickly examined the body and announced that he thought it had been in the water for at least two weeks. News soon spread around the village of the gruesome discovery, and a small crowd of locals turned up to have a look. With only one village constable to control them, they quickly gathered around the body.

"Oh my God, it's Maggie Munford," shouted someone in the crowd. Maggie was a well-known local girl, a drinking partner of Charlie Cartland when he made his occasional trips to The Kings Head pub in Farewell. Everyone knew she offered sexual favors in exchange for drinks or money, and that Charlie was one of her customers.

The investigation of the exhumed body was inconclusive. Charlie's body had shown no obvious signs of a struggle, so the family could have him reburied. With no other suspects for the murder, the police quickly decided that Charlie Cartland must have been responsible and had hanged himself in a fit of remorse.

"Makes it really easy for them, him not being here to defend himself," Frank heard Joan saying to John as he tried to sleep in the next room. John said nothing as usual; they all knew that most of the villagers were convinced that Charlie was the murderer.

The local, then the national, press arrived in the village wanting to know all about the Cartland family. For a few beers in the Red Lion, Charlie's old mates were happy to tell them what a drunk he was and how violent he could be. Charlie Cartland was depicted in the press as a monster, and with the police not inclined to pursue any more inquiries it became a simple case. It was accepted that Charlie Cartland had murdered Maggie Munford.

Life was miserable for the family. All of Frank's old playmates called him names: "killer's boy," "bad blood Cartland," and worse. Between Boxing Day and New Year's

Day, the family had been practically imprisoned in their cottage. Every time one of them ventured out they were assailed by questions from the crowd of pressmen. Fortunately by New Year's Eve, the press had had enough and all left to attend their celebrations.

Then, on the morning of New Year's Day 1910, another body was found. Frank believed that he was the first of the family to hear about it. To get away from the melancholy atmosphere in the cottage on New Year's morning, he had gone for a long walk up to and along the Devil's Dyke. Frank always found that this was the best place to escape the harsh reality of the real world. He normally had an optimistic nature, but that day he felt quite depressed about the future.

Still only ten years old, he found it very difficult to understand all the bad events that had happened in his short life.

It was a lot to cope with. He'd never known his mother, had a father who hated him and beat him regularly, and one who now everyone thought of as a murderer.

Wandering along the path through the gorse bushes and crimson-headed thistles on top of the dyke, he saw a huddle of people gathered round something in the ditch, about two hundred yards from the road.

Frank slid down the bank towards the group to get a better look. As he got closer he noticed one person he recognised. It was the small, plain-clothed policeman who had called at the forge cottage on Christmas Eve asking about Charlie. The Police Inspector noticed Frank coming down the slope and turned towards him.

"Hold on, sonny, you can't come any closer," he said.

Frank quickly turned left and ran back up the steep bank of the dyke.

"Hey, come down from there," shouted the Inspector. But Frank was too fast and upon reaching the top of the bank he peered down onto the scene below. There, lying in the long, rough grass, Frank could see a chalky white, naked body. Although it was lying face down, he decided it must be a girl because of the long, black hair.

"Get out of here, now!" shouted the panting Inspector as he struggled up the slope.

Frank did get out and ran the mile back to the cottage without stopping. He burst in as Joan and Edith were having a cup of tea.

"What on earth's the matter now?" asked a startled Joan.

"They've found another body up at Devil's Dyke," blurted a breathless Frank.

"Who is it this time?" Joan said slowly.

Frank explained how he had been chased away.

"Quickly go into the forge and tell John what has happened," said Joan.

"Can't you tell him?" asked Frank nervously. Over the previous few days he had become very afraid of John, who had started to look at him in the same way that his father used to. Joan came back from the forge looking puzzled.

"What's the matter?" said Frank.

"When I told him what you'd seen he just dropped his hammer and walked out," she said. Once more they sat around the kitchen table, lost in their own thoughts. It was almost dark when John arrived home. He had obviously had a heavy drinking session; they could smell the beer on him. But to their surprise he started talking - a rare event.

"That inspector and two other coppers came into the pub," he said in a slightly slurred voice. "One copper said they found the body of a woman and that she'd been murdered, recent like, strangled - same as that other old slag - so our old man didn't do it."

John swayed into his bedroom and slammed the door. The other children looked at each other with a nervous smile, not sure if it was through relief regarding the news or for hearing John say so much. Frank had never heard him string more than three or four words together before.

Over the following days, the cloud hanging over the Cartland family gradually lightened as news went around about the new murder. Frank smiled to himself when his friends all said they hadn't really believed his old man had done it. Never one to bear grudges, Frank accepted his mates' friendship back.

It was quickly discovered that the latest body was that of another well-known prostitute, Annie Hunt, from the nearby village of Morden. She worked part-time as a barmaid in the Prince Regent pub in Morden but was better known for her late -night work. She had been working at the pub two nights previously. This time the police had to look much harder for some evidence. They certainly couldn't blame the ghost of Charlie Cartland for this murder.

Two days later their Uncle Charlie rushed into the forge cottage.

"The police have arrested someone for the murders," he said. "I've just been in Newmarket and seen coppers leading him out of Merrywell Stables."

"Who is it? asked Frank excitedly.

"It's one of their stable lads, Ralph Stock. People say he has been acting strange lately. The lads said someone had reported to the police that they saw him with Annie Hunt on the night she disappeared".

"That doesn't mean he's guilty," said Joan, breaking into sobs, "they said father had been seen with that other girl on the night she was killed. I'll just be glad when this is all over."

The surly Ralph Stock had never been popular in Newmarket. He was a bitter and difficult failed jockey, whose wife had left him for another more successful jockey. Now he spent most of his meagre wages on gambling and drink. After being questioned unremittingly for two full days, he suddenly broke down and apparently confessed to the murders.

It was reported in the Cambridge Evening News that he had admitted he'd lost his temper both times and strangled the women when they had made fun of his height and bandy legs. Not much was said about how a five-foot, eight stone man had managed to move the bodies and dump them.

Ralph Stock was sent to Bedford Jail, with his trial date set for October. Although at the trial he denied ever admitting to the murders, the prosecution produced two fellow stable workers and Ralph's ex-wife as witnesses. The ex was happy to give evidence against him, stating that he often beat her up when drunk and had once tried to strangle her. The stable workers were two men Stock had crossed in the past and they were willing to swear that they had seen him with Annie Hunt only an hour before she disappeared. Although this was the only real evidence the prosecution had produced, it was enough for the jury and Ralph Stock was found guilty. He was hanged in Bedford jail on November 1st 1911, and both murder cases were closed.

The press had soon lost interest in the story just two weeks after Ralph Stock's arrest, and they moved on to more interesting news in London. In Houndsditch, there had been a number of shootings and three policemen had been killed. This soon made the events in Burlham of little national interest.

"Thank goodness that's all over and we can get back to our normal lives," said Joan as she put on her best coat and hat and went up to the church to give thanks.

The villagers of Burlham settled back into their everyday lives and quiet routines. The Cartland family, with considerable relief, went back to normal also. A few of their neighbours even apologised for the way they had treated them. January 1911 was exceptionally cold with sharp frosts and heavy snowfall. A blanket of pure, bright white snow fell over the whole village, endeavoring to wipe away the terrible events of the past December.

2

John, although only 17, was already six feet tall and weighed more than 13 stone. He had become a competent blacksmith, having worked alongside his father since a boy. His work was in great demand and he skillfully carried on with the family business. With the constant hard physical effort, he was growing very strong. Disturbingly for Frank he also looked and had started acting increasingly sullen, just like their father. I am going to have to be very careful around him in the future, thought Frank.

In looks and nature, Joe and Frank had taken after their mother's side of the family, many of whom were employed around Newmarket in the horse racing industry. Both boys had black, curly hair and were much smaller and slimmer than John; both had cheeky grins and optimistic natures. Their uncle Charlie was a successful jockey based in Newmarket, and although he never won any of the very big races, he had a sympathetic way with young racehorses that the trainers loved.

"The trainers all say I've got soft hands," he would joke with Joe and Frank, saying "but what do you two think?" after he playfully gave them a hard cuff around the ears. Frank and Joe both thought he was the father they should've had.

Some Sundays their uncle would visit to have tea with the family. He would often turn up driving a small cart pulled by a large goat. The boys were delighted to be taken for rides around the village in this strange contraption, and they proudly waved to all their friends.

Joe was now 14 and had left school. All he had ever wanted to do was follow his hero uncle Charlie and work with horses. On a warm April morning he excitedly came into the cottage.

"Uncle Charlie has found a job for me in Newmarket," he said. "I'm going to be a famous jockey." With his connections in horse racing, Charlie Willes had arranged a job for Joe as a stable lad in The Meddler Stud.

"You are going to have to work very hard in the stables mucking out and cleaning tack before they let you even ride a horse," said Joan.
Joan, like her brother John, had inherited their father's pessimistic view of life.

Frank loved his bigger brother Joe.

"I'm really going to miss you," he said as he watched Joe packing his canvas bag ready to leave. Joe always had a certain swagger and an air of confidence that Frank admired. He wanted to be just like Joe when he grew up.

"Frankie, my boy, you'll be fine. I'll never be far away from you, remember, just don't go doing anything to upset big John"
In fact, Frank carried on seeing Joe often, as Joe would turn up at home once or twice a month, cycling the three miles on an old bike his uncle had given him. He always brought his washing home for his sisters to sort out. Frank looked forward to hearing Joe's wild tales of his adventures in the rough pubs of Newmarket.
At least some of his tall tales must be true; Frank thought when Joe arrived home one Sunday with a black eye and two missing teeth.

The following two years were uneventful for Frank, if not for the other members of his family. His sisters were both courting local men. Norman Crowe had known Joan since childhood. Their mothers had been best friends and there never seemed any doubt that they would become a couple one day. Like all the other Burlham children, Norman had been very afraid of Charlie Cartland.

When Charlie died Norman wasted no time in visiting Joan at every opportunity, and they soon became devoted to each other. Norman was a tall, thin, shy young man. His gentle, easy-going nature meant he was the complete opposite to Joan's father and brother John.
But although John's drinking had increased, he was usually sullen and quiet, giving Frank no real trouble.

In March 1913, Edith married her sweetheart, Pat Summers, who was a stud manager at Snailwell Stud near Newmarket. Ten years older than Edith, Pat was a widower with two young children, his wife having died of scarlet fever in the outbreak of 1908. A cottage was provided with the job and Edith was happy for the opportunity to escape her family home.

"How are you going to manage two young children?" Frank asked earnestly as she packed her case to leave.

"After having to look after you and Joe all these years it's going to be easy," she said, giving his hair a ruffle.
After school and in the holidays, Frank and his mates would rush around all over the village, innocently startling the old folk of Burlham by climbing trees, fishing in the brook and scrumping apples from the local orchards. Somehow, though, Frank always knew he was slightly different from

his schoolmates. For as long as he could remember he'd had no fear. The experiences with his father had taught him that he could put up with anything life threw at him.

In the village, standing close to the cricket ground, was a massive old Canadian fir tree that had grown to over fifty-feet tall. For three generations many of the more daring local lads had tried to climb it, but usually lost their nerve, with the bravest getting just over three-quarters of the way to the top.

"I dare you to try and climb it, Frank," said Fred Coles in front of the rest of the village boys one hot summer's day.

"If I do, what are you lot going to give me?" replied Frank.

"No one's ever climbed it, so we are sure you can't," said Fred. The others nodded in agreement. That challenge was all Frank needed. He was halfway up in a couple of minutes. The gnarled and wide lower branches made it easy. Then it got difficult.

The branches became thin and spiky, and small, sharp twigs dug into his hands and scratched his arms. Frank knew that nothing except a fall would stop him. The boys on the ground below shuffled their feet, kicking the fir cones nervously.

"That's high enough now come down now, you'll kill yourself," a worried Fred shouted up to him. Thirty seconds later, swaying on one of the highest branches, Frank shouted down,

"It's great up here, I can see for miles, why don't you all come on up and join meee …"

The branch that Frank had his arms and legs wrapped around suddenly snapped. The boys all gave out high-pitched screeches as he started to fall. Being in the middle of the tree, his descent was halted by a large branch that stopped him half way down. Frank was left wedged in its V shape. He hung there, silent, and unmoving, all the wind knocked out of him. His chest was skinned, and his ribs were hurting like hell. Fred, in tears, turned and ran to the forge.

"The … the branch broke and Frank is stuck in the big fir tree," he cried to Joan the moment she opened the door.

"Is he hurt?" she whispered, then recovering she shouted, "John, come quickly,
Frank is hurt - and bring the big ladder with you."
About a minute later John came out of the forge shouldering a large, long ladder. With a worried Joan chasing after him, he rushed to the cricket ground.
With great difficulty, John reached up and lifted Frank out of the tree. With surprising gentleness, he carried him back to the forge cottage. Joan had already sent Fred off to fetch Doctor Jones. The doctor arrived thirty minutes later.

"He has broken a couple of ribs but should mend alright," said Doctor Jones as he bandaged Frank up. When he had left, Joan said: "you are a complete idiot, Frank Cartland, why did you try a stupid thing like that?"

"Because they all said I couldn't do it," said a grimacing Frank.
He had never felt quite in step with the boys around him. While they all seemed quite happy and content with their place in life, he wasn't.

"When I'm grown up I want to do more with my life than just working on the farms and then drinking in the pub," he would often say to Joan.

"Oh, Frank, you should know your place and just be content here. Look how happy your brother Joe is with the horses, you could be just like him."

Frank said nothing he already knew he wasn't going to work for someone else. He would do his own thing, but just now he had no idea what that was going to be.

Most of the time he didn't think about his being different from the other lads, but on odd occasions he felt that it was as if his brain was slightly ahead of his body, not by much, just a split second or two. It gave him a sharp wit and the natural ability to make most people like him. It also made him occasionally impulsive and clumsy.

"Why don't you think before you act?" Joan would often say to him after he had managed to break another cup or plate while helping her with the washing up.

There was one person who didn't seem to like him much at all, and that was stern old Miss Manners, his schoolteacher. Miss Jane Manners was not actually old. In fact, she wasn't much older than forty. But with her greying hair scraped away from her face and swept up into a tight bun, wide hips, large bosom and tweed clothes smelling of mothballs, she could have been mistaken for sixty. She had always lived with her arthritic mother, and now that she was in her sixties, Jane had to look after her too. She had been the headmistress of the village school before her daughter. No one seemed to know what had happened to Mr. Manners. The two ladies lived in their rambling and crumbling old school house just 100 yards from the school door.

Frank had never liked going to school, he was always daydreaming and in trouble with Miss Manners.

"Your silly boy, Frank Cartland," she would say.
"What good are you ever going to be if you can't even spell
simple words? Your brother John was just as stupid."
Spelling and reading had always been difficult for Frank and
soon lost interest in school, spending most of his time
wishing he were somewhere else.

*Only two furlongs to go in the 2000 Guineas at Newmarket. I'm
urging my horse, whip in my right hand. One, two smacks. I can feel
the surge as my mount reacts to my efforts. We are closing on the
leader! The smell of horse sweat and of leather is strong in my nose,
and the purple and gold racing silks are flashing in the sunlight. Come
on! One more effort and we are in the lead, just as the winning post
flashes past. The crowd is going wild with excitement. I have won the
race by a nose, riding the King's horse.*

"Frank CARTLAND, I am talking to you!"
Miss Manners and her spelling class brought him back to
reality.
Frank was fed up of always being in trouble, getting his
letters mixed up and being called stupid by Miss Jane
Manners. When the Easter break arrived, Frank walked out
of his classroom and decided he would never go back. Still
only 13, he left knowing that he was far from stupid. In fact,
he thought he was much sharper and brighter than most of
the other kids in his class. He was frustrated and just wanted
to get on with his life.
"What do you think you are going to do if you don't
go back to school?" Joan had protested when he had told
her he was not going back. Frank suddenly knew. Nearly
every grown-up in Burlham now had a bicycle.

"I'm going to repair bikes," was his sudden, confident reply.

When Miss Manners called out Frank's name for the register on the first day back after the Easter break, there was no reply.

"Where is Frank Cartland?" she said sharply to Fred Coles, whom she knew to be one of Frank's friends.

"He's not coming back, Miss," said Fred.

"Well, we will see about that," said Miss Manners indignantly.

After school that first day, Jane Manners went to the forge cottage to protest to Joan about Frank's absence. The moment Joan opened the door, Miss Manners said,

"That little brother of yours will be trouble, mark my words. He needs to be back at school where I can keep an eye on him."

Joan looked down at the angry little round woman in front of her and said slowly,

"I'm sure Frank will be just fine. At least he won't be any more trouble to you, so you can pick on someone else for a change. Now go away."

Before the red-faced teacher could protest, Joan had shut the door in her face.

Frank had been listening from another room.

"Thank you for sticking up for me, you look really satisfied with yourself," he said, coming in and giving Joan a hug.

"I am. I've wanted to put Jane Manners in her place for years," she said smiling.

Jane Manners had taught all the Cartland children and none of them had liked her very much.

"Now, if you've really left school you can make yourself useful around here. Start by washing those dishes and pans, and then you can clean the cottage windows". With no school to attend, Frank spent his time labouring in the forge, which he really disliked, and on the farms, which he enjoyed. He was disappointed that he had, so far, found no one willing to let him mend their broken cycle, but he continued to ask anyone he found with a bike. Eventually, fed up with him asking every day, the butcher Alan Pope said,

"Alright, let's see what you can do with this old thing, it's been in the shed for more than a year."
From the back of his garden shed, Mr. Pope pulled out a battered, old, black bike with a buckled wheel.

"Thanks," said Frank excitedly. "I'll make it like new."
With difficulty, he pushed the old, rusty bike back to the forge. In the evenings, when John had gone to the pub, Frank started work. He spent four hours on it each night, and by the end of the week he had rebuilt it entirely. He delivered a shiny black working bike back to the surprised butcher.

"Well done, Frank," he said, "here's a bob for your hard work."

"Thanks, Mr. Pope," said Frank.
Frank was delighted, as it was the first money he had ever earned.
Then it was back to work in the forge until he could find another broken bike to fix.
When the fire pit was roaring, the heat from the forge was oppressive and hot enough to blister your skin if you got too close to it. The constant noise from John's hammers striking the anvil was deafening. The hiss of hot metal being

dipped into cold-water buckets sounded like a basket full of angry snakes. If there is a hell this must be what it's going to be like, thought Frank as he wiped away the stinging sweat that constantly ran into his eyes.

The Reverend Sexton was always preaching that they would all be cast into the fires of hell if they strayed from Christian ways. Even as he worked in this hot, dark place, Frank didn't really believe a word of it.

A small piece of hot coal spat from the fire pit and burnt his hand. *I have had enough of this*, he suddenly thought.

"Hey, where the hell are you going?" shouted John as he watched Frank take off his leather apron and walk towards the door of the forge.

"Sorry, John, I can't work in here any longer, you'll have to get someone else to do your dirty work," replied Frank bravely.

"Well, fuck off you little runt," was the loud and sharp reply from his big, angry brother.

Frank managed to duck out of the solid oak forge door before a big black horseshoe smashed into it with a loud thud.

Back in the cottage, he explained to Joan that he had had enough of forge work and told her John's reaction to his leaving.

"I'll try to calm him down. I'm sure he'll get someone else to help, but make sure you keep out of his way for a while," replied a worried Joan.

Frank had no intention of going anywhere near his increasingly disturbing older brother.

3

Now that he had managed to escape the forge and John, Frank went to find more work with the local farmers, particularly enjoying the summer harvesting. Fascinated with anything mechanical, especially the new steam-powered threshing machines, he took every opportunity to help with repairs. A very fast learner, he soon had many of the villagers saying,

"Get Frank Cartland to help, he can fix anything". Following his success at rebuilding the butcher's bike, more people began to ask Frank to repair their bikes, and his reputation as a fixer grew.

Then Frank fell in love for the first time.

Farmer Albert Betts had a wire-haired fox terrier bitch called Lucky, who followed Frank all over the farm. In the autumn, Lucky had another litter of puppies, much to Farmer Betts' disgust.

"There are more than enough bloody animals around here already," he said to Frank, picking up an empty hessian potato sack. "I'm going to have to drown this lot."

"No, you won't" said Frank boldly snatching the sack from the farmer. "I'll find homes for them."

There were only three in the litter and Frank decided that it would be easy to find homes for the puppies. Anyway he wanted the smallest puppy for himself. It was the runt of the litter, noticeably smaller than its two bossy sisters, with coarse salt and pepper-coloured hair that stuck out at right angles all over his body. He also looked lopsided, with one little ear folded over and the other standing straight up. Looking down into the innocent, big brown eyes of this funny little dog, Frank said,

"Think I'll call you Spike." Spike jumped up and licked his face.

Frank did find homes for the two bitches. The spinster sisters of the local butcher, Mabel and Sarah Coles, had just lost their old dog and were delighted to give the puppies a new home.

At first the rest of the Cartland family were unhappy with the new addition.

"Another bloody mouth to feed," was John's reaction.

"He's only small and won't eat much. He can share my food," said Frank.

John just glared at him. Fortunately for Frank, his big brother had found a strong young local lad to help in the forge. John had told Frank,

"You were a lazy sod. This kid is a real worker."

Before long, Spike's friendly nature and funny looks won everyone over, even John gave Spike the occasional old bone. There was also an unexpected bonus from having Spike around - no more rats in the forge.

Rats were always a problem in the village, especially after harvest time. Large brown rats scurrying along the edges of buildings, in barns and even in the church were a common site.

Being a terrier, Spike was born to kill these rodents. Unfortunately, he would also chase anything else that ran away from him. Rabbits and cats soon learnt to keep well clear of him.

However an incident with Spike did cost Frank some money.

Spike's reputation as a rat catcher became widely known in the village, and one-day neighbour Will Cooper asked Frank to take the dog into his garden. Mrs Cooper had gone to collect the eggs early one morning from the nesting boxes and as she lifted the box lid, a large rat had jumped out. Rumour had it that villagers all over Burlham heard her screams.

"There's a rat's nest somewhere behind the chicken run." Will Cooper said to Frank. Now his wife's experience meant that he had to get rid of it, and fast. It didn't take Spike long to find the nest. He was soon scraping away, his front paws digging wildly, and throwing earth out in all directions behind him.

Uncovering the nest, Spike made short work of the mother. Grabbing the nape of the rat's neck, the dog violently shook it, breaking the neck instantly. After killing the remaining rats Spike was tired, panting happily and muddy, with a couple of bleeding rat bites on his nose.

"Well done, Spike," said Frank as he pulled him away from the remains of the rats.

"That's a good job finished. Let's go home for some tea."

They were just passing the front of the chicken coop when a nosey chicken poked its head through the bars. Instinctively, Spike snapped his jaws and bit the poor chicken's head clean off. Blood sprayed wildly from the headless bird, covering Spike and the neighbour's trousers. Mr. Cooper had just come out of his house to congratulate them.

Will Cooper's mood changed instantly.

"Get that dangerous little mutt away from here," he shouted after them.

Frank and Spike were already running for home.
Although he had been pleased to have gotten rid of the rats
Will Cooper, was very unhappy to lose one of his best
laying hens. Frank had to buy a replacement hen from
Albert Betts, but as consolation the Cartland family did have
a lovely, fat chicken for Sunday dinner that week.
Spike was given the parson's nose.

Two weeks later, Joe, on one of his trips home said,
        "Let's go down to the Railway Arms for a drink,
Frank."
The pub was next to the railway station, well away from the
main village. It was the place where all the village youngsters
went for a drink. The landlord, Dan Turner, had a flexible
approach to underage drinking and with the pub being away
from the centre of the village; it was easy to see when
Constable Clarke was on his rounds and cycling down the
road towards the pub.
Joe brought a pint of mild for himself and a half for his
young brother. Spike loved beer and had his own ashtray
full, which he lapped up.
Sharing a packet of pork scratching's with Frank; he was a
very happy little terrier.
Joe and Frank were sitting in the corner of the pub smoking
their Woodbines when the older one said,
        "How'd you like to earn a bit of extra money?"
        "Of course, I would, but what would I have to do for
it?" replied Frank a little warily.
        "Be the bookie's runner for our village," said Joe.
Growing up close to the Newmarket horse racing industry,
Frank knew what a bookie's runner was - he also knew that
being a runner was illegal.

"How much will I get?" Frank asked.

"That depends on how good you are," said Joe. Most of the villages around Newmarket used bookie's runners. They were usually young boys who would run around the village to collect money from the men, and a few women, who were looking to place a bet. The boys would then deliver all the bets to a local village pub. When he had all that day's bets, the landlord would send them on to their bookmakers in Newmarket.

Frank turned out to be a very good runner indeed, although he came close to being caught by PC Clarke on a number of occasions. Constable Clarke, as he would later admit, often turned a bit of a blind eye to Frank's activities. He liked an occasional bet himself and didn't agree with this law on restricting gambling.

Within a few months of being a runner, Frank had saved enough money to buy a rusty old green bike from Dan Turner. He then spent hours stripping the bike down, repainting it dark green with some paint he found in the forge, and then rebuilding it with his trademark attention to detail. On the front of the bike he fixed a wire basket for Spike to sit in. They didn't need a bell, Spike would bark at anyone who got in the way as they tore around the dusty village paths and lanes on the bike his brother Joe named 'The Green Flash'.

The freedom the old bike gave him opened Frank's world. Working hard, he became a bookie's runner for two nearby villages, as well as Burlham, although this additional work was to cause him some problems.

There was a lad called Tommy Dunn who lived in the next village of Farewell. He had been the bookie's runner for the village but was slow-witted and sometimes 'mislaid' a few bets. The landlords of the two Farewell pubs had lost patience with him and, after hearing of Frank's growing reputation; they sacked Tommy and gave Frank the job.

"I'll get that cocky little bastard, Frank Cartland, he's taken me bloody job," said Tommy Dunn to his mates.

The following Saturday morning, Frank and Spike came charging through the right-hand bend into Farewell. Frank was pedaling at full speed. There, in the middle of the road, was a large tangle of tree branches and on the bank nearby stood Tommy Dunn and two of his gang, Fred, and Sam.

"Watch this, he can't miss all those branches," squeaked an excited Tommy as Frank approached. Frank snatched on the brakes but couldn't stop. The rear wheel locked, and the bike swerved sideways. Poor old Spike flew out of his basket. One of the branches then went through the front wheel of the bike, locking it and pitching Frank over the handlebars. He landed hard on the road, with the bike crashing down on top of him. The brake lever caught Frank on his forehead and sliced it open down to his left eyebrow. There was a lot of blood. He lay there unmoving, dazed but conscious. Gathering his muddled thoughts, Frank decided he had had a lot worse. Tommy and his mates came down from the bank laughing. They gathered around the prone, dusty and bloody figure of Frank to admire their handiwork.

"I think you've killed him," said Sam a little nervously. Frank lay still. He had been in this situation before. Slightly opening one eye, he saw the dusty, scuffed toecap of

Tommy Dunn's hobnail boot. It was only six inches away from his face.

"Nah, he's only pretending, this'll wake him up," said Tommy as he lifted his foot to give Frank a kick.

Just in time, a very angry Spike arrived. He had been lucky: when he had flown he had landed in a soft mossy ditch. Unhurt, he'd scrambled out of it onto the bank. Looking around he saw the boys surrounding Frank and immediately launched himself straight for them - snarling, biting, and snapping at their legs. The three boys panicked and scattered, but not before Spike managed to get a few good bites into them. The best one had been into the calf of Tommy, just before his foot reached Frank. After chasing the boys right away Spike went back to Frank and started licking the blood from his face.

"Thanks for your help, old boy," said Frank as he slowly and stiffly pulled himself off the road.

Checking over his arms and legs, he found he was scraped and bloodied, but nothing seemed to be broken. He was inspecting his buckled front bike wheel as PC Clarke cycled around the corner.

"What the hell have you been doing, Frank? Have you knocked down a tree?"

When Frank explained what had happened, PC Clarke said adamantly:

"You leave that little bugger to me. Now get yourself home and Joan will clean you up."

Frank hobbled away, pushing his damaged bike with Spike trotting by his side.

I've got a spare wheel, we can be back on the road by Monday, he soon decided.

"What on earth have you done this time?" asked Joan when she saw her bloodied, limping little brother.

"Just fallen off my bike," said Frank. "I'll be fine."
But the concern for her young brother had managed to etch another worry line into Joan's forehead.
Frank would become quite proud of the scar on his forehead, which spread down to his eyebrow. It remained with him his whole life. Most of the time it was faint, but it turned pink and obvious whenever Frank became angry.

PC Clarke had cycled straight to the house of Tommy Dunn. He knew the way, having had to call there many times before. Arthur Dunn, Tommy's father, was well known to him. Occasionally he had to arrest Arthur for fighting on Saturday nights. This was often after a heavy session in the pub when he had won some money on the horses.
Tommy stood crying on the table in the Dunn's kitchen, while his mother bandaged up his bleeding leg.

"That bloody dog of Frank Cartland attacked me for no reason, it needs fucking shooting, "squealed Tommy.

"I'll go and finish off that scraggy little mutt," said his father, as he took his shotgun from the wall.
At that moment, PC Clarke walked into their kitchen.

"Hold on a minute, Arthur," he said, "put that gun down, unless you want some real trouble."
Then, despite Tommy's protests of innocence, Constable Clarke gave the Dunn family the true story. Tommy received a couple of very hard cuffs on the head from his father and peed his pants. He was then dragged crying upstairs to his room and his father locked him in for the rest of the day.

Tommy Dunn gave Frank no further trouble.

But there was plenty of trouble to come. 1914 arrived, and soon everyone's lives changed forever.

4

While Frank Cartland was growing from child to young man in an overcrowded cottage in a small Cambridgeshire village, George William Marshall was also growing up in a small village. But the similarity ended there.

George was being raised in the Marshall family's imposing Elizabethan Manor House, which stood at the top end of the Sussex village of Sefton.

Sefton Manor was a rambling, 300-year-old, 30-roomed house that was set in 200 acres of rolling pastureland on the slopes of the South Downs. The Lord of the Manor owned most of the tithe cottages in the village, with many of their tenants being employed by the estate. George lived in the Manor with his parents, Lord John William Marshall and Lady Victoria Marshall, and his twin elder brothers, Matthew and Stuart. George had his own nanny while the family employed 20 additional domestic servants.

Born on the 21st May 1901, five years after his brothers, George was a lonely child. His father had been MP for Chichester and was now in the House of Lords, as his father and grandfather had been before him.

George saw very little of his parents. Lord Marshall spent most of his time away from Sefton Manor at the family townhouse in Mayfair. His mother showed little interest in the young George, leaving his upbringing to his nanny and their many servants. All her attention was directed toward his spoilt and selfish elder twin brothers, who were the future of the Marshall dynasty.

Victoria Marshall had come from a wealthy old southern English family before marrying John Marshall in 1895. Her family roots went back to Elizabethan times. More impressive than that, the Marshalls could trace their ancestry back almost 1000 years, to the crusader William Marshall, 1st Earl of Pembroke. His yellow and green halved coat of arms, with its red dragon rampart, was proudly displayed throughout the manor. It was tradition that close to their tenth birthday, the sons of each generation of Marshalls would be taken to the Templar Chapel in London. There they would leave a drop of their own blood and place a kiss on the imposing cold effigy covering the stone coffin of their ancient ancestor, William Marshall.

George's formative years were very easy thanks to his full-time nanny, his governess and plenty of servants. He didn't have to think or do much for himself. By the age of nine he had grown into a slightly chubby boy and he had the 'Marshall look'.

Neither Victoria nor John Marshall was particularly handsome, and unfortunately, they passed these genes onto their boys. All three were thickset and round-faced, with high foreheads and flat chins. They had blond, straight hair, with slightly-heavy eyebrows and small grey/green eyes. Fortunately, the boys all grew to around five feet nine inches tall, which helped negate their less attractive features. The spoilt upbringing had made George quite lazy; He was also a solitary boy with no one his own age to play with.

His one constant companion was his Steiff teddy bear, which he had been given on his second birthday. George secretly named the bear Bertie after his father's brother. Uncle Bertie was the one person to show any interest in George.

The bear had coarse hair the colour of dark honey, long arms and brown, glass eyes. A wide, stitched black line made up its mouth, which was turned down at the corners, giving it a mournful look. From that second birthday onwards, George and Bertie were inseparable.

It was two days after his tenth birthday that George found himself packed off to boarding school. On the way to the school Lady Victoria took George to London for his stone kiss. As he reluctantly entered the cold, damp and silent chapel George whispered,

"Do I really have to kiss him, Mother?"

"Of course, you do, silly boy, it's your duty as a Marshall," his mother said as she pushed him towards the imposing coffin. Reluctantly shuffling across the grey flagstones, George climbed onto the box placed against the coffin. He leant over the stone beard and kissed the cold, stone lips to do his duty. Quickly his mother pricked George's right thumb with a needle.

"Ouch," cried George as she squeezed his thumb hard, forcing a large red drop of Marshall blood onto the grey praying hands of the effigy of his ancient ancestor. His duty done, Victoria, without a kiss or any sign of affection, led George out of the dark chapel and into the fresh, spring air. Waiting outside the chapel was James Bird, the Marshall chauffeur. He stood with the back door of the family Rolls-Royce open.

"Get in, George, I expect I will see you at half-term," said his mother.

Then, without another word, Victoria turned and walked away towards the Embankment.

The ruby-red Rolls-Royce Silver Ghost, with limousine body and tulip back, was registered number M46. It was James' pride and joy. With George sitting alone on the wide, leather back seat of the rolls, quietly sucking his sore thumb, James drove straight to Leamington Hall boarding school. As George gave Bertie, tucked safely inside his jacket, a comforting squeeze, a single tear ran slowly down his cheek.

George was almost asleep as the Rolls purred its way along the school's long, winding drive. The sudden crunching of tyres on gravel brought George fully awake, and with apprehension he looked out at the imposing red-bricked building as the Rolls glided to a stop.

"Enjoy yourself, Master George," said James as he opened the Rolls door for him. "I'll be back for you at half term."

James drove off, leaving George and his two small suitcases standing in front of the large, dark brown, oak front door of Leamington Hall. The door had a large black knocker shaped like a lion, but George couldn't reach it. As he stood looking up at the lion's head and wondering what to do, the door swung open. A short round lady with smiley eyes greeted him.

"Welcome to your new home, George," she said. "We have been expecting you. I am Matron Greaves. If you have any illness or worries, I will be here to look after you. While you are at Leamington, I will take over the role of your mother.

As George looked up into this friendly wrinkled face, he thought, *I really hope you are not going to be like my mother.*

At first, boarding school was a real shock for George. Being woken up at 6am every day and sharing a room with seven other boys. This was a complete contrast to his old life; He found it hard to adjust.

But, for the first time in his life, he had friends. At Leamington School he found that most of the other boys also felt dumped and abandoned by their families. That first night, as he lay silently in his small bed cuddling Bertie tightly, he heard sobbing.

"Why are you crying?" he whispered to Simon, the little boy in the next bed to him in his dormitory,

"I miss my mummy and my little sister," said Simon in a small, squeaky voice. George was suddenly surprised to realise that he didn't miss anybody.

"Don't worry, Simon, I'll look after you," he said.

Over the next three years, the lonely boys' mutual unhappiness bound them together as they grew into privileged young men.

By his second term, George had settled quite well into the school routines, and he grew in confidence.

With nothing to do back at the manor during the Easter holidays, he walked into the stables where James was changing the engine oil on the Rolls. An old magazine lying on the bonnet. caught his attention. It had a picture of a car on the cover.

"What's this about?" he asked James as he picked up the magazine.

"It's Autocar, a motoring magazine Master George. It tells you everything about cars and racing," replied James. Excitedly turning the pages, George said,

"Look, it's got pictures of Brooklands in it! My brothers have been there, and I really want to go. Can I borrow this please, James?"

"Of course, Master George, you can keep it."
On his return to Leamington School, George asked James to send him copies of Autocar whenever he could. He would spend hours reading and -reading the articles on Brooklands and all the fantastic European races. Unfortunately, to the detriment of his education, George found Autocar much more interesting reading than trying to understand Latin verbs.

"What is it that you're always reading?" asked Robin McApline, one of the boys in George's dormitory.

"It's Autocar, it tells me all that is going on in the motor racing world," replied George confidently.

"I know what's going on there. My father had a car built and has raced it at Brooklands," said Robin with a dismissive air.

"Really?" said George excitedly. "I'm going to be a racing motorist when I'm older".

"I am too," said Robin, "and I bet I'll be faster than you."
George his confidence suddenly deflated didn't argue with Robin, but in his dreams, he was always behind the wheel of a racing car, roaring around the Brooklands track and winning races.

Lord John Marshall was a member of the same London Club as Mr. Locke-King, who in 1907 had built the

Brooklands race circuit on his Weybridge estate, much to the dismay of his neighbours. John Marshall was a heavy gambler and, as bookmakers were allowed at the track, he was keen to attend this new form of gambling.

George was almost eleven years old when he was taken to Brooklands for the first time, and the memories formed that day remained vivid his whole life.

The morning of Sunday 5th May 1911 was the most important in his young life; he had been looking forward to it for weeks.

It was a warm but overcast when James brought the Rolls to the front door of Sefton Manor and George, dressed in his Sunday best jacket, shirt, and tie, climbed in. His father and brothers also travelled with him, but Victoria Marshall remained at home.

"I've been there once and can't imagine why anyone would want to watch those smoky, noisy things," she'd said at breakfast that morning. "There are enough of them rushing around our roads here in Sussex."

They travelled in silence. George, his nose pressed to the window, watched the dappled greens of the countryside drift by.

The twins had been to Brooklands before, but like their father they preferred horses to cars, so they had no real enthusiasm for the trip. Lord John soon fell asleep, his snoring much louder and harsher than the quiet purring from the Rolls Royce engine.

Arriving at Brooklands through the tunnel under the track and into the paddock transported George to a new, magical world. He had his first sight of the monster racing cars. His first glimpse was of a big, blue car as it powered into sight on the massive, white concrete bowl. It was a life-changing experience for any young boy, overpowering their senses with the unique rich and pungent smells of burning Castor oil and hot rubber. Especially impactful was the ear-hurting, flame-splitting noise coming from the unsilenced engines. George stood in the paddock captivated by the flames and smoke spitting from the open exhaust pipes of Charles Jarrott's 4.5 litre Humber.

He was completely bewitched.

With his brothers, George watched as A.J. Hancock, in his silver 16hp Vauxhall beat the half-mile record at 97.67mph.

"I am going to be a racing motorist when I'm older and drive a car just like this one," said George innocently to his brothers. They both laughed at him.

"You will never be brave enough to do that, Georgie Porgie," said Matthew.

"You even get scared riding your little pony," added Stuart.

It was true. George never felt in control riding his horse, but this was completely different. A racing car had pedals, levers and a great big steering wheel to control it - it wasn't just some animal with a mind of its own and thin, leather reigns to pull on. *I'll show you two*, he thought. Driving a racing car is what I'm going to do.

That day he joined many other young boys in the hero worship of these daring, larger than life Brooklands drivers.

Without telling any members of his family, George had finally persuaded chauffeur, James, to teach him to drive. He pestered James for months before he finally gave in. His chance came on a summer's day when his mother had gone up to London and his father and hated brothers had gone to the Goodwood horse races.

Propped up on two cushions, his first attempts caused the Rolls to kangaroo-hop along the drive. However, within an hour, he had mastered the basic controls and was full of confidence. Despite James trying to slow him down, he started causing mayhem at the manor, spraying gravel all over the gardeners and churning up the lawns.

"I want to spend my whole life driving fast cars," said George to anyone who would listen to him.

A week later, while George was in the middle of one of his "laps" of the grounds, his father arrived home. Noticing his young son peering over the steering wheel of the Rolls, he became red with rage.

The moment George saw his father he pressed the brake pedal hard and the Rolls slithered to a stop, leaving two large muddy ruts in the grass.

"What the bloody hell is going on?" Lord Marshall bellowed. "James, I hold you responsible for this madness. Pack your bags now. You are sacked."

George jumped out of the Rolls and ran up to his father.

"It's all my fault, Father," he said bravely. "I…I made James teach me to drive. Please don't make him leave; he's the best chauffeur we've ever had."

In fact, James had been the only chauffeur at the manor during George's short life. His father looked down at his youngest son with some surprise. It was the first time George had ever answered him back. After a long pause, he said:

"Very well, he can stay, but you are banned from driving the Rolls. If I hear that you have been driving it again, well, it will be the worse for you, and for him." Lord Marshall turned abruptly and went into the house. George had earned the respect of James.

"Thank you for your support, Master George," he said.

A few days later, James was driving George back to Leamington School when James said:

"In one of the stables, Master George, there is an old three-wheel cyclecar. It's not been used for years but I'll get the engine running so that when you come back at the end of term it will be ready for you to use. But not anywhere near your father."

"Thank...thank you, James," replied George. He was shocked and delighted it was the first time ever that anyone had offered to do something nice for him.

5

By March 1914, Frank had managed to set himself up as a cycle repairer. After some pleading from Joan, John had reluctantly allowed him to base himself in a small corner of the forge. Noticing Frank painting an old plank of wood one day in early March, John asked,

"What you're doin?"

"I'm making a sign for my new business," said Frank, holding it up proudly. The plank had a dark green background, with CARTLAND CYCLES written on it in bright yellow paint.

"You can't bloody write any good, so how'd you make it?" said John.

"Doctor Jones helped me," replied Frank.

"Just don't be getting that metal crap in my way or I'll flatten the bloody things," said John before stomping off to the pub.

Early one chilly April morning, Frank was repairing a broken bicycle in his corner of the forge when he heard the distinctive, sharp sound of a single-cylinder engine outside. Doctor Howard Jones had purchased a new Triumph motorcycle and was keen to show it off.

"That's the most beautiful thing I've even seen," said Frank, after rushing outside. Admiring the silver machine he added.

"It's a 4 hp 550cc type B model, with a fixed-belt drive, and it cost you £49."
Doctor Jones had been giving Frank motoring magazines, and Frank had learnt by heart all the details of each motorbike and motorcar.

"Frank, you already know more about the motorbike than I do," laughed Doctor Jones, "but actually it only cost me £45."

Momentarily depressed, Frank thought he'd never have enough money to afford a motorbike like that.

Doctor Jones had witnessed the treatment Frank had received from Charlie Cartland in those early years, and was amazed at the happy, hard-working young man he was developing into. Whenever he had the chance he would encourage Frank's interest in mechanical things.

"Come on, jump on the back, let's go for a spin," he said to the young man.

Without hesitation, Frank jumped on. Unused to the extra weight on the back, Doctor Jones slowly moved off. Frank was soon urging him to go faster.

Buzzing with excitement from this first motorised experience, Frank realised that bicycles would never again be quick enough for him.

By July 1914, everyone knew that the war with Germany was a reality, but in the small country villages of England it had little immediate impact. The war was just something that was happening hundreds of miles away, across the sea. almost another world.

Frank's business of repairing bikes continued to grow, and when the Triumph engine broke down, just a day before his birthday, Doctor Jones allowed him to rebuild it.

"Here's an early birthday present for you," he said.

"See if you can fix it."

Frank dismantled the damaged engine, and with the new parts Doctor Jones had purchased, lovingly rebuilt it with great care. He refitted the engine into the frame of the

Triumph and nervously, with Doctor Jones, John and Joan looking on worked the kick-starter. The engine burst into life instantly.

Joan sighed with relief as Doctor Jones jumped on and roared off to test it. He had been gone for more than ten minutes when Frank started to worry. Then, with great relief, he saw the silver Triumph reappear around the corner. Doctor Jones stopped the bike in front of them and, with a great smile on his face, said:

"Amazing. Frank it runs better than ever. You have magic in your fingers." John walked away in disgust.

At that moment Frank realised that building engines was what he wanted to spend the rest of his life doing.

"I just love being able to create a living, breathing machine from all those cold, metal bits," he enthused to Joan and anyone else who would listen.

"But look at your fingers, Frank, you have cut them to ribbons on that sharp, hard metal," said Joan with concern.

'That's fine, doesn't hurt. I'm always going to leave a bit of my blood behind when I build an engine. It will show it's one of mine!" Frank laughed.

The army recruitment campaign didn't reach the shires until 1915. An Army brass band arrived in Burlham on a hot August Saturday.

"Come and look at the band and soldiers," said an excited Joe, who had come home for the weekend, to his sister Joan. She was in the outhouse doing the family washing.

Reluctantly she joined the rest of the excited villagers as they gathered outside the village hall to hear the band perform.

When the band had finished playing their stirring marching tunes, an immaculately dressed sergeant major addressed the happy crowd.

"We are here to offer all you fine young men the opportunity to join all the other brave English soldiers. To come and fight for your country to defeat the Hun," he proclaimed in a commanding voice. Then, smiling at the captivated crowd, he added:

"And remember lads, every girl loves a man in uniform."

He pointed to a handsome young sergeant seated behind a trestle table that had been set up on the corner of the lawn. All single men of 18 and over were encouraged to sign, although conscription would not come for another year. Of course, Frank being just 15 meant he wasn't old enough to sign up.

Much to the distress of Joan, her sweetheart Norman Crowe and her brother Joe excitedly joined the long queue of Burlham young men. Despite Joan's pleading, within the hour they had both enlisted and joined the Cambridge Regiment. Seeing his sister cry always upset Frank. To lighten the mood he said,

"At least you won't have to do Joe's smelly washing for a while."

This set off a new wave of tears from Joan.

Norman and Joe had become great mates, even though Norman was four years older than Joe. They all knew he loved Joan and one day would pluck up the courage to ask her to marry him.

"When I was your age, Norman took me down to the Railway Arms for my first drink and gave me my first Woodbine," Joe had told Frank.

They were happy to go into the army together and were looking forward to the adventure. Of course, none of these boys and young men had any idea of the horrors they would soon have to face.

"Have to learn me some French if I'm going to chat up some of those lovely French girls, but don't worry, sis, I'll look after your Norman," said Joe, giving Norman a sly wink and Joan a big hug. Norman just kept quiet; his mother was standing next to Joan, and she was also distressed and crying. Suddenly he took Joan's hand and said,

"Joanie, when I come back will you marry me?"
With tears streaming down her cheeks Joan said,

"Of course, I will Norman Crowe, you silly man. I love you." Then she hugged him until his ribs hurt.

"I'm going nowhere, it's not bloody worth it," said John, much to Joan's relief.
He knew he had responsibilities at home, and he was always working long, hard hours in the forge. But really, he had no intention of giving up his evenings in The Red Lion drinking … one of many ways in which he was increasing like his father.

Two months later, Frank stood silently, Spike sitting next to him. His crying sisters and sullen brother alongside him, as Joe and Norman proudly marched away. The boys all looked so grown up in their new army uniforms, their shiny black polished boots and the metal on their brown rifles glinting in the weak autumn sun. The column of fine, young men filed past and Joe shouted over his shoulder,

"Look after our sisters, Frank, we will be back soon, so don't worry about us."

An unsmiling Norman waved and blew Joan a kiss. They would never see Norman again, and Joe would come back as a stranger.

After training in Yorkshire, the Cambridge Regiment of around 50 officers and 1000 men crossed the English Channel to France in January 1916. Joan had been receiving letters regularly from both Joe and Norman, and from the tone of the letters they were both in very good spirits. Joe's letters, of course, were full of optimism and told of his adventures with the French girls.

Norman's letters were more restrained and described the countryside and weather, but what he did say was how much he was missing Joan, that he loved her and couldn't wait to get home. He always referred to his fiancée as "my Joanie".

In the last letters she received in May 1916, Norman had said that all the boys in the regiment were getting excited because they had been told they would soon be moved to the frontline on the Somme. That was the last letter Joan received from her boys.

Joe and Norman were looking forward to some action. They had been training for months and, together with all their comrades, were desperate to do their duty - without question. The regiments were moved up to the front on the Somme during June. The snaking column of thousands of men marched to the constant, deafening sound of artillery. For weeks, the German lines had been shelled mercilessly. The British commanders were supremely confident, to the point of arrogance, that the constant bombardment would have severely weakened the German forces.

They were certain that the German frontline would not be able to resist the new planned offensive.

Evidence of that arrogance came when an order was sent down the lines that when the whistles went for the attack the British troops were to walk to the German lines.

"Sounds like this is going to be easy," said Joe to some of his mates when they heard about the order.

Early on the morning of 1st July, Joe and Norman stood together nervously waiting.

"Get ready," the call came from their sergeant.

The friends crushed their last, half-smoked Woodbines under their boots into the soft, grey, trench mud. Then clasped hands and smiled at each other.

"Don't forget you owe me a beer, it's your round when we get home," said Joe. "I bought the last one at the Railway Arms."

Norman grinned but he was not smiling when, with his hand still tightly held in Joe's, he said:

"Tell Joanie I love her."

"You can tell her yourself when we get back mate," replied Joe, but he had also stopped smiling.

For more than a minute there was complete stillness and silence along the lines. It was as if the thousands of men were holding their breaths. Suddenly, the silence was broken by a hysterical shriek as hundreds of whistles blew all along the line.

En mass, thousands of young British men rose up and went out onto the stark grey muddy wastelands to start their walk of death.

Joe slipped on the wet mud as he left the trench, but Norman didn't. The moment he stood to start the advance he was hit by a hail of machine gun fire. His body danced like a demented stringed puppet then, falling sideways, his body smashed into Joe. The impact knocked Joe back down into the trench. As he fell backwards, his head crashed into the wooden walkway so hard that his skull fractured on impact. He was instantly knocked out.

He'd been saved from the slaughter by his dead best friend.

And slaughter it certainly was. Within minutes, thousands of dead and desperately-injured men lay upon the once-green fields of the Somme. A monstrous German scythe had instantly and totally felled the fresh, green shoots of British youth.

When the medics eventually found Joe he was still unconscious and completely soaked in blood. Lifting Norman's lifeless body off him, they could see his chest moving and they gently placed him onto a stretcher. With so much blood covering him, they were convinced he must have a major injury somewhere.

At the field hospital, all Joe's blood-soaked clothes were carefully cut away, but no injuries were found. All the blood had belonged to Norman Crowe.

The newspapers back in England that week were full of the headlines.

"Our boys slaughtered"

"Massacre on the Somme"

With no news from Joe or Norman, or any of the other boys who had left with them for that matter, the whole village of Burlham was in limbo. The residents spent each day just waiting and thinking the worst.

"I know we won't see them again," said Joan constantly.

The worry and stress had seen her lose almost two stone in weight. She had hardly eaten or slept since the last letters from her boys.

"Their letters will probably have been lost," said Frank, without much   conviction. "I'm sure we'll hear from them soon."

For most of the women and girls in the village, the short walk up the hill to St Mary's church became a daily ritual. Joan spent many hours in the family pew just praying. Her knees worn red raw by the constant kneeling on the cold stone church floor.

It was 28th July when the letters arrived. The dawn had brought a beautiful, clear, blue summer's morning sky. It was also Frank's 17th birthday.

Joan saw the postman's bike approaching and let out a low moan, as if she knew he had a telegram for her that would begin, "we regret to inform you ..."

John ran out and snatched the letter from the postman and tore it open.

"He's not dead," was all he said, handing the letter to Joan.

"What does it say?" asked Frank. He was desperate to know what had happened to his brother. With a trembling voice, Joan read,

"Private Joe Cartland has received a serious head injury and is in a French hospital." Excitedly, she added, "They will be sending him home in about two weeks."

Putting the letter down, she burst into happy sobs.

They all looked at each other with relief; even John managed a slight smile.

But it was just two minutes of happiness. Their mood changed the moment Norman's mother, a hysterical Mrs.

Crowe, burst into the cottage. The letter she waved confirmed that her son, Joan's sweetheart, had been killed. This was the letter Joan had been expecting.

Frank would forever remember the tears and sorrow that lasted throughout his terrible birthday. It was a scene played out in so many towns, villages, and hamlets throughout Great Britain in that most somber of summers. Cricket on the sunny village greens held no attraction that summer. Many villages didn't even have enough young men left to form a full team.

Twenty thousand men and boys were killed on that one-day, 1st July 1916, at the Somme. Five of those were from Burlham.

The extreme emotions Joan experienced in those few minutes - finding out that her brother was still alive and that her lover was dead - were too much and caused her complete collapse. She never really recovered from that day, although through necessity she continued to look after the Cartland household as before. Joan had never been an optimistic person. Circumstances meant her whole life had to be devoted to others. Her life was never her own. The rest of her family always took priority.

Now her one chance to find happiness for herself had gone, and any lightness of spirit she previously felt left her forever. Norman Crowe's body never returned to his home village. He was buried along with thousands of other young men in one of the many war cemeteries close to the Somme. The Reverend Walter Sexton organised a memorial service for Albert and the four other Burlham boys killed in the war. The whole village attended the service where a brass plaque was dedicated and engraved with their names. It was placed on the right-hand, inside wall of the church, close to the Cartland pew. This, at least, gave Joan and the other families some comfort and a focus for their grieving.

Frank had always loved Joe. He had admired and looked up to him his whole life. When Joe eventually arrived home two months later, Frank was shocked to see that only the shell of the cocky, happy young man who had marched away so confidently just one year previously remained.
It broke Frank's heart seeing the change in his brother, who sat silently by the kitchen range day after long day, not talking, and just gently rocking back and forth.
"I can't bear to watch him, I want the old Joe back," he said to Joan.
"I know, we all do, but at least he is alive," she said with a bitterness Frank hadn't heard before.
"Sorry, Joan, I didn't think. I know you miss Norman badly."
Joan said nothing. She just gave Frank a big, long hug.
Doctor Jones, into whose care Joe had been placed, explained to Joan that when Joe fell back into the trench his head had fallen directly onto the end of a large broken wooden stake. Skull fragments had been pushed into his brain and would be lodged there for the rest of his life. No one could be sure just how much of his brain had been damaged, or how much of a recovery he would make.
For the first time in his life, Frank experienced emotional pain, then real anger, as he witnessed the distress this war had brought to his family and the families of his friends.

All his life, he had looked forward to spring. It filled him with optimism, especially the sudden explosion of golden daffodils waving in the warming sun. Almost overnight they would banish the memories of winter, as they turned everything yellow, spreading their bright light haphazardly throughout the village. But this year the three to four-week lifespan of these beautiful flowers held little joy, their short, bright life depressed him.

Only Spike managed to bring back something of the old Joe. Spike would often sit with him - it was as if he could sense Joe's pain. Often, he would jump onto his lap and lick his face. This usually brought a rare smile to Joe's lips.

"Why don't you take Spike for a walk?" said Frank to Joe one bright, April day. To his own and Joan's delight, Joe had replied,

"I ... I think I will today, come on old boy."

"Don't go far," said a worried Joan.

Two hours later, the family was becoming concerned. There was no sign of Joe or Spike.

"I'll go and look for them, I think I know where they would have gone," said Frank, jumping onto one of his bikes. He cycled through the village and out towards the Devil's Dyke.

These ancient earthworks dominated the landscape for more than ten miles, and they divided the parishes of Burlham and Farewell. The Devil's Dyke ran through the racecourse at Newmarket Heath and provided a good and popular view of the racing. Frank reached the dyke and noticed the black outline of Joe and Spike on the skyline. They were walking towards him. Frank was relieved to see Joe looking so happy, with Spike panting at his side. Greeting him, an excited Joe said:

"We walked along to the racecourse and watched some of the horses. Spike has been chasing rabbits."

A walk to the racecourse would become a regular event for Joe and Spike in the following years, but Joe never became mentally fit enough to work again.

On bad days, severe headaches would confine him to his bed, and these became more frequent in later years.

Frank did occasionally suffer a pang of jealousy since Spike had transferred most of his affection to Joe. But he had to smile one day as he watched the pair wander off down the lane to the Railway Arms for their daily ration of beer. As they went, Spike turned his head and looked back at Frank, as if to say, "Don't worry, I'll look after him."

Early one November morning a dusty and bruised Doctor Jones walked into Frank's workshop.

"I left the old Triumph outside for you, Frank," he said.

"It's got damaged forks this time. I've fallen off for the last time. If I ride it again I'll probably kill myself, so it's about time I got a car instead. You can have the bike."

"Are you sure?" Frank asked. "I'll pay you for it."

"No, that's not necessary, but you can give me a free service on the car when I get it," Doctor Jones replied.

Frank couldn't help himself. He gave the doctor a big hug. "Careful lad my ribs hurt enough already", the doctor had protested.

Frank soon had the Triumph running sweetly again and took every opportunity to ride it. Before long he had become a skilled rider and an expert repairer of motorbikes.

Rushing around the villages and country lanes of Cambridgeshire became a drug to him. The freedom and excitement this gave him was unequalled by anything else he had ever experienced.

He knew, of course, about the daring exploits of the racing motorcyclists at The Isle of Man and Brooklands, having absorbed all the motoring magazines supplied by Doctor Jones. Now he had just one ambition in life - to join them.

6

By 1917, with the war showing no sign of ending, Frank was determined to enlist. He felt a strong need, in some way, to avenge Norman's death and the mental destruction of his brother. But he knew it would be difficult telling his sister.

"You are so selfish," protested Joan. "Hasn't there been enough pain in our family already? You are too young, not yet eighteen and only older men are being conscripted."
"I'm sorry, Joan, it's…it's just something I need to do," replied Frank. Despite Joan's despair and protests, he was determined to enlist.
Although he didn't want Frank to go to join the war, Doctor Jones had heard that there was a need for motorcycle dispatch riders in the army. He called on Joan and Frank at the forge to tell them.
"I thought that it would interest Frank if he is still determined to sign up," he said, looking at Joan.
"That sounds really great, it would be the best job for me," said Frank   excitedly.
Joan said nothing for a while, but she was thinking that this must be safer than being an ordinary infantryman like Joe and poor Norman had been.
"Thank you for your interest, Doctor Jones. If that's what Frank wants, I can't stop him," she said with tears welling in her eyes. Howard Jones' instinct was to put his arms around Joan. But his shyness caused the moment to pass.
Howard managed to find the right contacts in the army and Frank was soon signed up as a dispatch rider.

On 1st August, just four days after his eighteenth birthday, Frank arrived in France.

Reporting for duty at the motor pool, he was issued with his army motorbike. Frank was delighted that it was a Triumph Model H Roadster, widely known as the "Trusty Triumph". It was obvious that the bike had seen plenty of action already - its army green paint badly chipped and scarred with what looked like shrapnel marks.

"Who was riding this old thing before me," Frank asked his sergeant.

"Never you mind, sonny, it's your bike now. All you have to do is ride the bloody thing." This was all his superior would say. No one else seemed to know the bikes history either...or else they were reluctant to tell him.

Doing the thing he loved best, Frank had impressed the army instructors with his riding skills, his complete lack of fear and his engineering expertise. His reputation quickly became widespread and he was often given the most hazardous assignments.

The daily routine of taking dispatches from the British Generals' château headquarters, which were safely behind the lines, to the frontline trenches became second nature to him. At the frontline, he had an introduction to the terrible destruction and the squalid conditions three years of war had already brought.

At night he would lay in his narrow bunk unable to sleep because he was thinking about the horrors all around him. Now knowing how his brother had felt, he thought. How can anything be worth all this misery and pain?

One dispatch gave him many sleepless nights and left him with memories that would remain with him all his life.

It was dusk the grey light fading fast. Frank had been riding through driving, cold rain and German shelling became particularly heavy as he approached the frontline.

Unable to see more than a few yards he decided to take
shelter. Frank stopped the bike outside an abandoned old
barn that had somehow survived the shells which had
destroyed the farm-house which had once stood next to it.
He stepped inside the dark building, relieved to be out of
the rain .his eyes struggling to adjust to the darkness.
The barn had no windows, only a small shaft of light came
from a jagged hole that had been blown into the roof. Frank
had walked two paces into the dark barn when the
overpowering smell hit him like a punch in the face. It was
all the worst smells of his childhood - a mix of rotting meat,
shit and piss. Then he heard a noise which sounded like the
neighbour's pigs back home feeding in their pen. He turned
on his army torch.
In the far corner of the barn he could make out movement
and took out his pistol. The beam of light from the torch
settled on a site of nightmares. Six or seven large brown rats
were feasting on, and in, the remains of a human body. He
could just recognise the dark-blue uniform of a French
infantryman. Frank lost control and hysterically fired his
pistol into the heaving mass. The rats scattered, and, in the
torchlight, he watched a swarm of big, black buzzing flies as
it appeared, snake-like, out of the body.
Retching, Frank turned and staggered out to his Triumph
and, despite the falling shells and hard, driving rain, he
started the engine and roared away. After that experience
the sight of any rats or large, black flies would always fill
him with disgust and horror.

One week later, still unsettled and depressed after the
encounter with the rats, an unusually dry day saw him riding
through a badly-rutted road that followed a small river.

The beat of the single cylinder Triumph engine was constant as he scrambled along the uneven track. Frank's mood was reflected by the words hammering through his head.

Noise, mud, blood and death
Noise, mud, blood and death
Noise, mud, blood and death
and the beat went on and on...

Frank was hot, depressed and extremely tired. The slimy mud had dried in places to become gritty, grey dust. It had invaded his clothes, his eyes, his nose and his hair.

To his left he noticed the sun twinkling on water. Between the trees flashing by he could see a small silver river - no more than twenty feet wide - flowing with a slow current. Braking to a stop, Frank got off the Triumph and leant the bike against a willow tree growing at the edge of the river. Its long branches were caressing the clear, silver water as it flowed past. He was surprised to find the willow tree made him think, for just a fleeting moment, about his father and cricket. Then the thought had gone.

The water looked irresistibly inviting. It was the first time in the six months he had been in France that Frank had seen water without light-grey scum, dead horses and bloated bodies floating along it. Within seconds he had stripped off his dusty clothes and was naked. The bank was steep and slippery, so he was careful as he slid down into the clear water. The water was icy cold and no more than four feet deep at its centre, but he didn't care. Diving down, he immersed himself, feeling free and clean for the first time since leaving England.

As his head came clear of the water, he opened his eyes and noticed a young woman standing on the bank. She was under the willow tree next to his clothes, and she was watching him. For many seconds they stood staring at each other, and then she said,

"Bonjour, parlez-vous Français?"

Frozen and struck dumb, Frank stood as the current of the water flowed around the thighs of his shivering body. He tried to hide his manhood with his hands, though actually with the icy water it was more like his boyhood, and he needed only one hand to hide his embarrassment.

Frank had picked up the odd word of French and coming to his senses, he replied,

"Bonjour, Madame, mon nom est Frank."

"Mon nom est Marie," replied the girl. She was smiling as she speedily stepped out of her dress and slip. Naked, she slipped down the bank into the water and slowly walked towards Frank. Marie was about five feet tall and very slim. Her auburn hair was long and curled up as it rested on her shoulders. Conker's, thought Frank, her hair is the colour of conkers. It had been his favorite game as a boy. He once had a tenner, which he retired after it won ten brutal contests. He had removed its string and placed it carefully on the ledge above the range in the forge cottage kitchen. I wonder if it's still there, he thought.

Next moment he was being splashed with cold water. Marie was close to him now, and her infectious light giggle made him laugh for the first time in years. He noticed that his new friend's smile seemed to take over her whole face and that her small, firm breasts had dark brown, hard nipples. She came closer and continued to splash him. Frank splashed her back before grabbing her. They fell together under the water and spent an idyllic few minutes playing and laughing in this magical stream.

Marie took his hand and led him back to shore. They struggled up the steep slope before she pushed Frank down on the bank under the lime-green leaves of the old willow tree. The long soft grass enclosed him like a glove. Marie opened her legs and slid down on top of him. He could feel the hard bone above her dark, brown-haired mound pressing into him. Her hair, smelling of wood smoke, enclosed his head like a canopy. Urgently she rubbed her wet body against his, her bullet-like nipples pressed, almost painfully, into his chest. They gradually warmed each other and, as she moved, riding him like a horse, Frank quickly became hard enough to enter her. He lost himself in the exquisite experience. As she moved her ride became a trot, which soon became a canter, which then became a furious, reckless gallop. When Frank exploded inside Marie, his mind was in one of those moments after climax, when nothing else exists or matters in the world.

He fell asleep in the grass for a moment, then, suddenly, the harsh real world once again crashed in on him. It was the thunder of a new artillery barrage. Frank opened his eyes to find he was lying alone and naked on the riverside bank. There was no sign of Marie. He had no idea where she had gone; it was as if she had never been there at all.

Dressing and riding back to the Chateau, he found he had lost two hours.

"Where the hell have you been?" said his sergeant.

"Dirt in the carburetor again, had to stop, strip the bloody thing down and clean it," said Frank. The sergeant had very little knowledge of engines, so Frank knew he would not question him. That night in his narrow bunk he was unable to sleep. The endless pounding of the continuous heavy

British artillery shelling of the German lines rang in his ears, but the scent of wood smoke also lingered in his hair.

Frank had signed up as a dispatch rider for one year, or until the end of the war. His year was a few weeks from being completed when he killed a French deserter.

There were many of these men roaming the countryside. Thousands had deserted after the Battle of Verdun. The war had turned some into savages who were becoming almost as dangerous to the Allied troops as the Germans. Returning from the frontline after eight hours on duty, Frank had been riding the old Triumph steadily down a dusty lane just one mile from his base. Only a hot meal and a night's rest were on his mind.

Without warning three, tramp-like, figures, dressed in the remains of blue uniforms, jumped onto the lane just 100 yards ahead. Frank saw that at least one of them had a rifle, and it was pointing at him.

Skidding to a halt he turned the Triumph through 180 degrees and twisted the throttle fully open. Accelerating away he felt a punch into his left shoulder, it spun him off the bike and onto the gravel of the lane. The poor Triumph continued rider-less until it veered off the lane and destroyed itself against a substantial elm tree.

Shaken, but largely unhurt apart from his left shoulder, Frank looked up to see the four ragged men moving cautiously towards him. His right hand had already opened his holster and his fingers gripped the pistol inside. When the armed and apparent leader of the group was no more than 10 yards from him, Frank drew his pistol and fired. The shot hit the man in the middle of his forehead and he dropped like a stone, face first, onto the gravel. Before

Frank could fire another shot, the other three deserters fled into the trees.

Looking down at his shoulder, Frank could see that a bullet had gone straight through his arm. Surprisingly, there was very little blood, and he was relieved to see that the bullet appeared to have missed any bones. He dragged himself up onto his feet and hobbled over to the dead French soldier lying face down on the lane. A trickle of bright red blood from the soldier's head formed a rivulet in the dry, grey dust. Frank turned the body over with his boot. He remained there for a few seconds before sinking down and sobbing at the side of the body. Before him, staring up with sightless eyes lay a young boy of no more than seventeen. Doesn't even need to shave yet, thought Frank, as he gently closed the boy's eyes. Tears came as he sat in the middle of that dusty lane, with the boy's head cradled in his lap. Frank's thoughts were of home. He remembered watching his sister Joan sitting alone and silent for hours at the white, old pine table as she waited for news of their brother Joe and her beloved Norman. This boy's mother must be sitting somewhere in France waiting for news of her son. With his one good arm, Frank easily dragged the French boy's body to the side of the lane. It feels like a bag of bones, he thought.

He shuffled slowly, in mental and physical pain, back to the château. He could see why his brother had returned from this war destroyed. All this wasted life filled him with anger, but he was determined not to become a victim. If he survived, he was going to be happy and make a success of his life.

The injured arm ensured Frank's war was over. Within one month he was shipped back to England and arrived home at the forge to a tearful and emotional Joan, a smiling Joe, and an over-excited barking, jumping Spike. He even received a sullen "welcome home" from John.

7

Of course, death shows no favours to rich or poor, and the Marshall family was to experience more than their fair share of the sorrows inflicted by the "Great War".

Just like for Frank miles away in East Anglia, the start of the war had no real impact on George or the villagers of Sussex. Quite happy at school, and although he wasn't outstanding at any subject, he was less lonely than when at home.

He arrived home at the end of the spring-term in 1916, and was surprised to find both his father and mother present. But Lord Marshall had not come home to see George. He was there to say farewell to Matthew and Stuart.

The twins had recently joined the Royal Sussex Regiment as officers. The following day they were leaving for France. Dressed in his best formal clothes, George travelled in the Rolls Silver Cloud to the station with his parents to see his brothers' board the train for France along with the rest of their regiment.

Victoria Marshall had been distraught when the twins announced they were joining up, and she had tried desperately to stop them going. But it was no use, peer pressure and the need to uphold family honour made their recruitment inevitable.

George lined up with his parents as Stuart and Matthew formally shook hands with each of them. George thought how young and scared they looked, as his father shook their hands in turn he said:

"Remember your crusader ancestors; don't let the family name down. Go out there and fight for your country." Looking up into his mother's face George could see no sign of emotion as she also shook her son's hands. There were no hugs. No tears. The contrast with the emotional outbursts of the other mother's waving their son's farewell was acute.

White steam filled the platform as the train slowly and noisily pulled away from the station.

George did feel a momentary pang of guilt that he was happy to see his brothers disappear into the distance, but like the train that feeling soon disappeared.

Two months after his brothers had left for France, George was struggling through a Latin lesson when the headmaster walked into the classroom. He made his way directly to the teacher and whispered in his ear. Both men looked straight at George. The headmaster beckoned George to go with him. All the other boys watched in silence as George slowly got up from his desk and followed the headmaster out of the room.

As they entered the headmaster's study, George noticed Matron Greaves was already there, sitting in a corner.

"George, please sit down," said the headmaster. "Would you like a glass of water?"

"No thank you, sir," said George softly.

George had an idea about what was coming next. One of his classmates had been called to the study two weeks earlier.

In a low, grave voice, the headmaster said,

"Unfortunately, I have some grave news for you, George. Both of your brothers are dead, they have died doing their duty for the King, for England, and for Leamington School."

George felt his legs fold under him as he collapsed onto the floor and whispered,

"What… Surely not both of them?"

"I'm afraid so, I've been told they died together, fighting bravely for our country like so many of our other old boys."

Matron Greaves helped George up and guided him back to her rooms, where she made him hot sweet tea.

James arrived at the school in the Rolls a few hours later to take George home.

"Sorry to hear about your brothers, Master George," said James as he opened one of the passenger doors.

"Thank you, James," was all George could think to say as he stepped into the car.

Alone and silent in the back of the Rolls, with just his faithful Bertie for company, a single tear ran down his cheek once again. Not in sorrow for his brothers, whom he had never liked at all, but because this time he realised that his life had changed for good. He was the only remaining son and now held the full responsibility for the Marshall family future. He knew his mother wouldn't let him forget that. He did have the wit to think; well at least she will take some interest in my life now.

Matthew and Stuart Marshall were both killed on 18th July 1916. On this terrible day, the Royal Sussex Regiment lost 17 officers and 349 men. Stuart had watched with horror as his brother was blown apart in front of him. Without pause he had continued his charge across the cratered wastelands until he was felled by machine gun fire from the German lines.

This tragic day would always be known as "The Day the Sussex Died".

8

In rural Cambridgeshire, a year after the war ended, Frank had become very successful at repairing the local bikes, motorbikes and even a few of the cars that were starting to become more common on the village lanes and byways. With the business growing rapidly, he employed two young local lads to help.

His injured arm had now fully recovered. Frank had returned from the war a hero, but he hated this glorification. The war had destroyed the lives of too many people he loved. His war medals were thrown to the back of a drawer in his workshop and forgotten about. They were never to be displayed or talked about. The death and the horrors Frank had experienced in France would never leave him and he saw no reason to be reminded of those terrible times.

New interests were gradually helping him get over those dark days.

Now nineteen years old, he had made his girlfriend Margaret Foster pregnant.

Margaret, the only daughter of village baker Reginald Foster, had always felt that she and Frank had been childhood sweethearts, but she had always been keener than Frank. Margaret would follow him and his mates everywhere as they grew up. Frank always tolerated her, but he had shown no real interest.

By the age of seventeen, Margaret had bloomed into quite a pretty young woman. At five feet four inches tall, she was only four inches shorter than Frank. She had light-brown eyes the colour of ripe walnuts, dark-brown hair, freckles on her small, upturned nose, and a shapely figure.

Her mouth turned down slightly in the corners, which unfortunately made her appear rather unhappy, but this disappeared when she smiled.

Frank's war experiences had certainly caused him to grow up. Like many of his fellow survivors, he never talked in any detail about those experiences, but later in life he would often think back and inwardly rage about the terrible and stupid waste of life that the war had caused.
Encouraged by Joan, who thought a girlfriend would help him settle down instead of roaring around on his motorbikes all the time, Frank started taking a serious interest in Margaret.

In the hot summer of 1919, early one evening after helping with the harvesting, Frank and Margaret found they were alone. They lay together in one of the haystacks that they had just helped farmer Albert Betts to build. The work had given them a real thirst and they had both managed to drink two large glasses of the homemade cider the farmer had given them.
Over the previous months, Frank had often taken Margaret down to the Railway Arms for an evening drink. On the way back, they would sometimes stop in the playground of the village school they had both attended a few years earlier. The bench there was known as the "courting bench", and here they had tentatively been exploring each other's bodies. Now, as they lay hand in hand and giggling under the warm evening sun, Frank surprised himself and said,
        "I love you, Margaret."
In response, Margaret smiled and said,

"Good, I love you too. I think it's time. I want to feel you inside me now."

Smiling at him, she sat up and unbuttoned her shirt, freeing her firm, round white breasts. Excitedly, Frank gently squeezed the right one before greedily taking the dark brown, stiffening nipple of the left breast into his mouth. Moaning, Margaret quickly pulled down Frank's shorts and underpants, releasing his rapidly-stiffening cock. In one swift movement, she lifted her skirt and kicked off her knickers.

Grabbing his cock, she pulled him on top of her. Unfortunately, things were happening far too quickly for poor Frank, but as he tried to control himself Margaret held him fast, parting her legs and stabbing him inside her. This exquisite sensation was too much for Frank. He shuddered and came almost immediately. Embarrassed, he pulled out and away, quickly sitting up in the straw. Pulling bits of straw from his curly hair, Margaret, still giggling, said:

"Don't worry, Frank, you can practice every day when we are married."

Married! That word came as a real shock to Frank and sobered him up immediately. He certainly hadn't thought about marriage before.

Two months later he had to. Margaret came into the forge while Frank was on his knees struggling to repair some bent forks on a customer's bicycle.

"Isn't it wonderful, I'm going to have your baby," she said, laughing.

Margaret was both excited and delighted. All she'd ever wanted out of life was a husband and children.

Now she was about to get both. A shocked Frank slowly put down the hammer he was holding. While still on his knees he said,

"I expect we will have to get married then!"

"If that's your proposal, Frank Cartland, I accept." said a happy Margaret, "And I'll get Daddy to find us a house. Now, let's go and tell everyone."

In fact, Frank was not too upset about the prospect of marriage, as he desperately wanted to escape the depressive atmosphere at the forge. With an increasingly unpredictable John, a silent Joe and a religious, nervous Joan living there, he had started to dread going home each evening.
Frank had prayed earnestly before his father's death, but he didn't really have faith in any religion.

"How can there be a God?" he would say to Joan.

"No God would allow the evil I've seen in this world."
Joan had no answers, but she needed to believe in something. Frank was also aware that he needed a lot more space for his growing motorcycle business. He could see that marriage to Margaret, with her father's family money and help, would be a great opportunity for him.
Two weeks before the wedding, Frank, in a mild panic, said to Joan,

"I've got nothing to wear for the wedding and I don't know anyone who has got a suit."

"Why don't you ask Doctor Jones? I'm sure he will have one," Joan replied
Frank went to see his friend and borrowed a brown suit. The only trouble was that it was about two sizes too large.

"It's going to look rather big on you," said Howard Jones, "but I'm sure Margaret won't mind."

Meanwhile, Margaret's father had indulged her. Her aunt made her wedding dress to a pattern of the latest fashion. It was cream in colour with frills on the bodice, wide, puffy 'gigot sleeves', a long train and a veiled hat. Her two little nieces, daughters of her brother Thomas, were to be the bridesmaids.

Frank wanted Joe as his best man, but it was clear that Joe would not be able to manage the job. So instead he asked his old school friend, Fred Coles.

Once again, the villagers walked up the hill to St Mary's church this time to celebrate rather than mourn. A mixed selection of guests gathered there. The few Cartland family members and Frank's friends did their best to fill the right-hand pews, while the left-hand pews were full in numbers and in size. As the majority of the three generations of the Foster family were bakers, they were round, loud and jolly people.

It was a lovely autumn afternoon as Frank, with the organ starting "here comes the bride", turned to watch a slightly-plump Margaret happily walking down the aisle at her father's side.

The moment he said,

"I will", Frank, for an instant, thought, what am I doing here?

Then he was swept away by events, following the familiar rituals as if they were a dream.

After the confetti and bouquet had been thrown, caught by Margaret's cousin Sally, the wedding party walked back down the hill. As they did so the wind increased, wiping a shower of brown leaves from the beech trees, which covered Frank and Margaret.

"Isn't it wonderful," said Margaret with her arm firmly around Frank's waist, "it's like walking through a golden snowstorm. This is the happiest day of my life."

The reception was held in the Burlham village hall, with the Fosters providing a substantial wedding spread and a four-tier wedding cake. The Red Lion provided the casks of beer and cider. Unfortunately, as often happened, the beer was the downfall of John, by 8pm he had had far too much of it. Margaret's cousin Sally had been sitting quietly on her own. She was resting after a few dances with her friends. In common with six of the other single women at the wedding, she had lost her sweetheart in the war. All weddings were now hard to cope with, just a constant reminder of what she had lost. Still only twenty-five, she was putting on a little weight, but was still pretty and had not lost hope of finding a husband.
John, the beer giving him courage he didn't normally possess, moved unsteadily across the room, and sat down next to her.

"You look lovely tonight, Miss Sally," he slurred. "Will you come outside and give me a kiss?"

"No, I will not, John Cartland, please go away, you're drunk!" Sally replied.

"Why not? My stupid little brother is good enough for your cousin, so I should be good enough for you," said John loudly.
Reaching over he tried to put his big hairy arm around Sally's shoulder. Sally's younger brother, Dick, having watched as John approached his sister, rushed over and grabbed John around the neck, pulling him onto the floor. It should have been an uneven fight as John was at least

four inches taller and two stone heavier than Dick, but the surprise attack and too much drink took John off guard. Dick landed a punch square on John's chin, but the impact hurt his fist far more than it hurt John.

They continued to throw wild punches at each other, neither inflicting any real damage on the other, until eventually they were dragged apart, and the fight petered out. Slowly hauling himself up from the floor, John staggered outside and, to everyone's relief, didn't come back.

Joan went to a worried looking Frank and said,

"I expect he will go home to his bed now. Don't let it spoil your big day."

The mood soon lightened, everyone getting back to enjoying the reception. Even Joan, who would usually go and make sure her 'boys' were all right, soon forgot about John. She was dancing and enjoying herself for the first time since the war.

Overall it was a successful wedding day. A slightly-merry Margaret continually told everyone that it was the happiest day of her life. The couple spent their first night together at The Rutland Arms in Newmarket. It was a wedding gift from Frank's uncle, Charlie Willes.

Frank made up for his lack of control two months earlier.

"Oh Frankie, you really are my man," sighed Margaret, as they made love for the third time that night.

The next morning at 9am, after the happy couple had enjoyed a full fried breakfast, Charlie Willes arrived with his pony and trap to transport them back to their new home,

Ivy Cottage in Burlham. They were a happy, carefree couple as they shook and bumped in the back of the trap.
They had just three miles of happiness. When they arrived at the cottage a nervous-looking Joan was waiting outside.

"I can't find John anywhere," she said, "and Sally hasn't been seen since she left the wedding reception to walk home last night. I'm worried sick."

"Have you been to look for him at the forge?" asked Charlie.

"No, I can't get in, the door is locked, and I can't find the key. I shouted through the door but there was no answer," Joan replied.

"I expect he is inside sleeping off his hangover," said Frank. "I keep a spare key under my bed in the cottage; I'll go and get it."
When they tried the large key, they found it wouldn't go all the way into the keyhole.

"It's locked from the inside, the key must still be in the lock," said Frank.

"We'll have to break the door down," said Charlie. "I'll get some help."
A few minutes later, Charlie came back with Constable Clarke, who had been riding by; also with them was Margaret's father, who had been on his way to greet the couple at their new home. By this time both Margaret and Joan were very distressed. They sat crying in the back of the trap.
Constable Clarke found a heavy sledgehammer, which he and Mr. Foster took turns to swing and slam into the heavy, black oak door. But the lock was doing its job too well and their efforts had little impact.

"We are going to need something much heavier to get through this bloody door," panted Charlie.

"Frank, run to Albert Betts and tell him we need to borrow his steam hammer."

Five minutes later, Frank came back with Albert. They were both struggling to carry the heavy instrument.

A large crowd of villagers had gathered around to find out what all the noise was about.

"Go away, there's nothing to see here," Joan shouted at them, which of course made them even more curious. Once enough pressure of steam had built up, Albert Betts directed the piston at the heavy door. Releasing the holding catch, the hammer thundered into it and the black wood splintered. With a sound disturbingly like a woman screaming, the great door gave way.

The site that greeted them was one Joan and Frank had seen before. This time it was their brother hanging from the great beam, not their father. Joan collapsed immediately. Margaret and some neighbours carried her back to the cottage. Frank, remembering scenes he had tried to shut out for years, just turned and ran away. He didn't stop until he reached the sloping banks of Devil's Dyke.

Tom Clarke, Charlie, and Albert Betts went inside the forge and shut out everyone else as best they could with the shattered door. Charlie found a big, old brown tarpaulin in the corner of the forge which he managed to hang over the lintel of the door.

Between them they managed to untie the end of the rope and gently lower the lifeless body of John Cartland down onto the dirt floor of the forge.

"I'll go and get Doctor Jones," said Albert Betts, wanting a reason to escape the nightmare. On the workbench in the corner of the forge, Tom Clarke noticed a large poster advertising the funfair that had visited Burlham two weeks earlier. He walked over and picked it up. He was about to screw it up and throw it away when he noticed black smudge marks on his fingers. Turning the poster over he saw that the plain white back of the poster had writing on it in thick charcoal.

"Come over here, Charlie, and look at this," he said. With great difficulty they began to read;

"It's me what done for them two old slags, the old man helped me get rid of the first un, but couldn't handle it an hung hisself. Now i gone too far, couldnt help meself when the urge comes cant control it didnt mean to kill poror Sally   just wanted her t love me. you all beter orf witd out me."

At the bottom was a sprawling signature, which could have read John Cartland.

Frank sat in his favorite spot high on the bank of the dyke under two gorse bushes. They always protected him from the worst of the wind, which often howled across the great green earthworks.
This was the place he always came to when he needed to escape the bad times. Spike had followed him from the village and now sat panting at his side. From here they could see for miles. To his left, just one mile away, was the huddle of houses that was Burlham, with the top of the church towering above them. Sweeping his gaze right he

saw the vast, flat fenlands, a straight line stretching away until it hit the large full stop that was the cathedral on the Isle of Ely. On a clear day he could make out its spires ten miles in the distance.

Frank suddenly realised that he hated John. Even though he had no knowledge of the note his brother had left, Frank felt sure he knew what his hanging body had meant, he must have hurt Sally.
He had never really hated anyone before, even his father who had beat him so badly. Frank felt that there was a good reason for all his anger.
He thought of poor Joan, whose whole life had been blighted by those around her. From the moment their mother died, Joan had been a victim of other people's actions. He knew today's events would finish her and he felt helpless to ease her pain. Thankfully Joe wouldn't be able to understand what was happening all around him. Frank rather envied his brother stuck in his own little world.
At least Edith had the good sense to get away from this cursed family, he thought.

As he sat there, and the sun briefly came out from behind the high clouds he decided that he was not going to be a victim, no matter what had happened or what would happen next. He was determined to make a success of his life.
Frank knew that there was a desire that had put a fire inside him that nothing could put out his love for speed. Racing along the Cambridgeshire roads on the fine edge between disaster and glory were the only times when he felt completely alive.

News of John Cartland's death had gone around the village like wildfire. With the arrival of the Inspector of Police from Cambridge, it wasn't long before the press started, once again, to descend like vultures on the unfortunate Cartland family. Sally's very angry brother and father were soon at the remains of the forge door demanding to know what had happened to their girl. When they realised that Sally's body wasn't in the forge with John, they organised a search party. The scene was chaotic, with a couple of local police trying to keep control.

The crowd had rapidly become an angry mob that wanted some answers. If John Cartland hadn't already hanged himself, the mob would have done the job for him.

Margaret, just one day into her married life, was back at her family home being comforted by her mother and father. The honeymoon was certainly over.

From his vantage point on the slopes of the dyke, Frank could see a line of people approaching. He walked down to meet them.

"What's going on?" he said to Margaret's brother, Dick, who was leading the train of locals.

"We are searching for my sister," Dick replied. "We think your bastard brother has killed her, you Cartlands are all murderers." Noticing Spike at Frank's side, he added, "even your bloody dog is a killer."

They all pushed past Frank, even his best man Fred Coles, almost knocking him over. Just twenty-four hours earlier these same people had been shaking his hand and congratulating him, now they spread out to start their search along the dyke.

As Frank watched, the ragged line slowly disappeared away from him he suddenly realised that Dick was right; he was a murderer, twice over. He was responsible for the deaths of the poor French soldier and his mother, who had died from giving birth to him.

Head down, he and Spike started a slow, lonely walk back to Burlham to face the drama and sadness that he knew he would find at the forge. The happiness and laughter of yesterday seemed like a lifetime ago. Arriving home, he pushed his way into the cottage through the growing crowds gathered outside. He sat down at the kitchen table where his uncle and Doctor Jones were already seated. Joan and Joe had been given sedatives by Howard Jones and were lying in their beds.

"Sorry, Frank, it looks like your brother has hanged himself and he's left a note," said his uncle sadly.

"What does it say?" asked Frank.

"John says he was responsible for both the old murders as well as for killing Sally," said Charlie.

"But that can't be true, they hanged the guy who killed the other two women, didn't they?"

"We all thought so, but it looks like John has confessed to those murders as well," Charlie explained. This was far worse than Frank had expected. Not only had he lost a brother, but now the nightmare with the nation's press would start again.

With the Cartland family cottage once again under siege, Joan, Joe and Frank stayed together inside for two days. Joe, who didn't understand why all the noisy people were outside, became very agitated.

"I want them to all go away," he said. "I want to take Spike for a walk. And why isn't John here?" he would repeat the same questions almost every hour.

When Doctor Jones brought them necessary supplies, he also gave Joe some more sedatives to ease his distress. Joan and Frank sat in silence for hours.
As they all expected Inspector Davies arrived, Frank noticed that his hair and pencil-thin moustache had turned almost white since they had last met him before the war.

"We need to know if John had any special place where he may have gone last night," he said, looking directly at Frank.

"Don't know of any," Frank replied. "He spends, I mean used to spend, all his time either in the forge or down the pub."

"Well, if any of you think of anywhere be sure to let one of the constables know. I'm keeping two on duty outside to stop the press pestering you all."

"Thank you," said Joan dully.

For two full days, from first light until darkness enveloped the countryside, a dozen policemen and most of the villagers continued their search for Sally, but no trace of her was found.
On the third morning, Constable Tom Clarke was cycling past the cricket field when he decided to stop and take another look. It had been one of the likeliest places that John would have gone but had been searched on the first day. The Pavilion had been built on the far side of the field, away from the road. It was only a simple three-roomed hut, with a home dressing room, an away team dressing room

and the main area where the scorers sat and the teas were served. When he entered it was empty, as he had expected. Walking outside, he went to the back of the pavilion and tripped over a wooden ladder lying in the long grass. *What do they need a ladder for down here?* He thought.

Then, looking up at the tiled roof, he noticed a small porthole window in the pitch of the building. Excited, he realised that there must be a room up there. He was dragging the ladder around to the door of the pavilion when two local lads turned up.

'What are you doing with that ladder, Clarkie?" asked one of them.

"PC Clarke to you, cheeky little sod," he replied, before adding, "give me a hand with this, we need to find the trap door into the roof."

They discovered it above the door in the visitors' changing room. It was flush with the ceiling and almost unnoticeable. Tom Clarke leant the ladder against the doorframe and went up. He pushed the hatch upward with ease and poked his head through the gap. A dim light directed a beam from the east facing porthole window.

Highlighted on the floor of the loft lay Sally's body.

"Anything up there?" shouted one of the lads.

"Both of you run up to the village and get a message to Doctor Jones. Tell him we need him here urgently."

With the boys running off, Tom pulled himself up into the loft and crawled across to Sally.

She lay, fully clothed on her back and with her hands clasped together across her lap. Sally looked as if she was sleeping, but he could clearly see the ugly, purple bruises around her chalk-white neck.

The national press once again based themselves at the Red Lion pub and, much to the landlord's joy, drank the place dry. Reporters spent their time investigating all areas of the Cartland family, covering their pages with sensational, upsetting headlines. "Like Father like Son" was one of the most common. No one seemed to bother much about the fact that poor Ralph Stock had been hanged for two murders that he hadn't committed.

The old Charlie Cartland suicide story had been dragged up again and given comprehensive coverage alongside that of his murderous son, John. The Cartlands were front-page news for a few days but following the release of the confessions in John's suicide note and the discovery of Sally's body, there was little fresh news to report on. The press gradually drifted away and lost interest in the village of Burlham and the remains of the devastated Cartland family. They moved on to find fresh new sensationalist stories.

All Margaret had ever wanted was to have a normal family life, but it was a very difficult start to their marriage. Many of Margaret's relations wanted nothing to do with the Cartland family, and most of the villagers were, for a while at least, wary around Frank. *Surely, they can't really think I'm like him?* He thought to himself sadly.

With pressure from Margaret, they had persuaded her doting father to buy Ivy Cottage and its' orchards, which were just one hundred yards down the high street from the forge.

Old Mrs. Grange had recently died age 75, having lived in the cottage for 40 years, so the place was very run down. The roof leaked due to broken and missing slates, and it really was Ivy Cottage, being covered in the invasive green plant. The clutch walls were crumbling and unstable in many places where the ivy roots had made their home. Frank didn't mind hard work. In fact, laboring all day helped to stop his worries, and he soon made the place habitable for his new family.

After three months' hard work, when the house was fit for Margaret to move into, he started on his workshop. He wasted no time and soon built a large garage on the plot of ground next to the cottage.
Already Margaret could clearly see how her new husband's mind worked.

"You have spent more time working on that garage than finishing the cottage, she protested.

"There's still lots more work to do in our home."
But Frank was impatient. He was ready to expand his business. The new sign went up, again in golden yellow writing and with a dark green background, and Frank began trading as CARTLAND MOTORCYCLES.
The most difficult time came when he had to move all his bikes and equipment from the forge. It was the first time he had entered since John's death. He rushed in and pulled his bikes, engines, spare parts, and tools outside before slamming the repaired door shut with relief. The atmosphere inside the dark, old forge could only be described as menacing.
Frank hoped he would never have to go in there again.

He felt very guilty as he packed up all his things, leaving Joan and Joe alone in the sad, quite cottage, with only bad memories for company.

Spike was putting on weight. He spent most of his days keeping Joe company rather than being outdoors exercising and it seemed that Joe had lost what little confidence he had built up prior to John's death.

Just seven months after Margaret and Frank's wedding, Margaret went into labour. When her waters broke and splashed on the kitchen floor, Frank was in his workshop across the yard. She staggered to the cottage door while screaming,

"Run to your grandmother's, Frank, and be quick." Agnes Willes now 68 years old, was still delivering the Burlham children. It took just five minutes before she arrived at Ivy Cottage with a worried Frank at her side.

"Just stay out here, Frank," said Agnes as he tried to follow her inside the cottage. A nervous Frank lit another Woodbine and went back to his workshop.
He tried to finish rebuilding the engine he had been working on when Margaret had first screamed at him. He hammered and tapped as loud as he could to drown out the sounds of Margaret's pain coming from the cottage.

An hour later his grandmother called out to him.

"You can come in now, Frank,". With relief he dropped his spanner and ran into the cottage. In their bedroom he saw a tired but smiling Margaret cradling their healthy baby girl in her arms. It was such a relief for him. Since his own birth had killed his mother, all childbirth filled him with dread.

"Can I hold her?" he asked.

"Of course you can, stupid, she's your daughter," said Margaret softly.

Taking the tiny bundle gently from her he looked down at the shock of black curly hair and the round, pink face. The baby's brown eyes were open and looking straight up at him. Frank suddenly understood that there had been a fundamental change in his life; nothing would ever mean more to him than this tiny girl.

"Let's call her Mary, after my mother," he said as tears flowed down his cheeks.

9

Sexual experience for George had come much earlier than it had for Frank. Arriving home from school a day early for his summer holidays, in the carefree years before the war began, he had been excited as he rushed into the library. The latest copy of Autocar was in his hand. He intended to spend the afternoon absorbing the reports of the recent Tourist Trophy races on the Isle of Man and the latest Brooklands race meeting.

Upon opening the library door, he came face to face with Sally, one of the kitchen maids. She was on her hands and knees and hard up behind her was his grunting, red-faced brother, Stuart.

For an instant George thought they were playing a game, but he soon realised what was really happening. He had watched the family prize bull servicing the heifers in the farmyard, and Sally had the same blank, sad and resigned look on her face as those cows.

George turned quickly and had his hand on the doorknob about to leave when Stuart noticed him and said,

"Hey, Georgie Porgy, don't go. Come over here, it's time you learnt how to do this."

Stuart made two hard thrusts into Sally and let out a low grunt. Slowly and reluctantly, George moved into the room and stood next to his elder brother.

"Now it's your turn, pull your trousers down and stand here," he said to George. Nervously George did as he was told. Unfortunately, although he felt some small stirrings in his little cock as Stuart roughly pushed him into

Sally's hot, sticky backside, George was not ready for this experience. He stood shaking and unsure what to do next. He was about to cry when someone said,

"Here, Georgie let me show you how it's done."
It was his other brother Matthew. George hadn't noticed him sitting in an armchair watching him with amusement.

"My Sally needs a real man," he said, pushing George aside. Forcing Sally's legs apart he thrust his already-hard penis inside her.

"There!" he exclaimed, "that's how to do it, Georgie." He pulled out and playfully slapped Sally's pure white, round bottom.

"Thank you, Miss Sally," he said. "Now get back to work." Sally quickly straightened her skirts, stood up with difficulty and slowly walked to the door. She had not uttered a word.

The twins walked out of the room laughing and joking soon after Sally. They left George alone within the walls of the dark, leather books. He still had his trousers around his ankles.

Six weeks later, the Marshalls were at dinner in the dining room at Sefton Manor. Lord John Marshall was sitting at the head of the large, dark oak table and directly opposite him sat Victoria Marshall with their twin boys.

Stuart sitting on her left and Matthew on her right. George had already been driven by James back to school for the new term.

They had finished their course of minestrone soup and sat in silence waiting for the delivery of their roast beef. Suddenly, the door burst open and a large, middle-aged woman rushed in. Liz Porter was assistant cook in the Marshall household. She was also Sally's mother.

Liz jumped onto the oak table, scattering the wine glasses and table decorations everywhere. She kneeled in the middle of the table and, with her backside facing Victoria, lifted her skirts to reveal her fat, round arse. Her bottom was hairy and pockmarked, with two large boils dominating the left cheek. One boil was an angry red while the other was larger and purple, with a creamy white top.

It was a volcano ready to explode.

"Why don't you take me like you did my poor Sally," she screamed at the two scared-looking twins.

"Tell you what; you can have both ends, one each."

Liz opened her mouth to reveal two rows of yellow and black teeth. Turning to look straight at Victoria, she added,

"Make sure you keep these chinless shits away from my girl in future.

All this happened so quickly that initially none of the Marshalls had time to react. Now Victoria came to her senses and screamed,

"Get this old hag out of here."

The butler and two servants rushed in and grabbed Liz. Before she was dragged kicking from the room she shouted back,

"I see you all enjoyed the soup. You should, I poured the remains of my overnight chamber pot in it when cook wasn't looking."

Liz was crying as she shook off the hands holding her and walked out of the room.

For minutes, the Marshalls sat in shocked silence among the mess. The quiet was eventually broken by the sound of Stuart retching. No one wanted roast beef.

Victoria was next to make a sound. Her face was crimson with rage.

"What have you two been doing to her girl?" she shouted at the white-faced twins.

"Quiet woman," boomed John Marshall, "sounds like they have only done what the male Marshalls have done for generations - buggered the servants - it's what they are for!" He gave the boys a knowing wink. Victoria stared at all three in turn and stood up with a look of total disgust on her face, sending her chair crashing to the floor.

"You all sicken me," she said and stormed out of the room.

George thought about that time in the library with Sally many times over the following years. Later, after his brothers' deaths, he remembered that two other young girl servants, as well as Sally, were no longer working in the kitchens.

"Where did the maid Sally go?" he had asked James one day.

"She was sent away like all the other girls carrying your brothers' bastards," said James with considerable anger. George decided not to ask more questions.

The death of the Marshall twins had not been mourned by any of the Marshall servants. Most of the staff had lost good men from their own families in the war, and they certainly had no room in their broken hearts for those two boys.

Victoria Marshall now focused her attentions on her only remaining son, much to George's discomfort. She had been utterly distraught at his brothers' deaths, but this was no ordinary mother's distress - she had invested twenty years of her life in their futures. That wasted time devastated her. Initially, she had moved herself away to the South of France for eighteen months. Her parents' family owned a large, rambling villa just a mile outside Nice. It overlooked the Mediterranean Sea and she retreated there in the hope it would help her recover.

The end of the war saw Victoria move back to Sefton Manor. She had just one aim, to turn George into the next Lord Marshall and to make sure that the family line continued.

With his mother away and his father continuing to spend most of his time in London, George had been free to develop his passion for driving. The experience and the excitement of his visit to Brooklands were etched into his brain. Driving the small cyclecar James had rebuilt for him was great fun. He pretended he was Charles Jarrott, his Brooklands hero, as he charged around the farm fields in the little machine, although he did manage to scare himself a few times by going too fast and almost turning over.

James sometimes watched George driving from a distance. *That boy is never going to make a successful racing driver,* he thought. *He's too afraid of hurting himself.*

On her return from France, Lady Marshall wasted no time in looking for a suitable wife for George. For many generations, sons of the Marshall family had been sent to Trinity College, Oxford, to complete their schooling. The twins would have followed this path, but now there was only George.

Victoria was quite happy to accept Leamington School's advice that academically George would not be suited to university life. She had other plans for him anyway.

Apart from the need to ensure an heir, she had discovered that her husband, whom she knew had at least two mistresses, was an addictive gambler. He spent as much time at the Newmarket and Goodwood horse races as he did in the House of Lords, and he had recently lost a large amount of money on the horses.

Victoria had received a great shock when she arrived home from France to find their butler Sykes packing the family silver into a large box.

"Sykes, what do you think you are doing?" she asked.

"Lord John has instructed me to list and pack all this silver, my lady," he replied.

"We will see about that," she said and went to find her husband.

"What the hell are you doing with the silver," she demanded when she found her husband in the library.

"I've had a bad run on the horses lately. My luck will turn when I pay off my Bookmakers," he replied sharply. Victoria realised that any protests from her would only provoke anger, so she remained silent and walked out. The experience left her with a new determination that George would need to marry for money, as well as to a good family - and soon.

10

"Fearless" Frank Cartland had, by 1921, become a successful motorcycle race rider. He had developed his riding skills around the fields and roads in the Fens and, of course, as a dispatch rider during the war. He started riding in trials events, but these were too slow for him and he very soon progressed to motorcycle hill climbs and road races. He was given the nickname Fearless Frank due to his attitude to danger.

Having very little money, Frank had no choice but to build all his own motorbikes and engines. His success meant other riders were soon very keen to pay him to build their engines also.

"Do you have to go away every weekend?" Margaret complained. "It would be nice if you could spend some time here with Mary and me for a change."

"I have to race myself to prove how good my engines are," replied Frank.

"But what you are doing is very dangerous. You have responsibilities now and a family that needs you here," said Margaret, becoming tearful

Following a recent race, Frank had made the mistake of telling Margaret that one of his fellow riders had been killed. The reality was that he now needed the adrenalin rush that the race riding was giving him; this had become the most important passion in his life. He knew Margaret was right, but rational thought would always come second when the alternative was speed.

Frank's continued success insured that the motorcycle business was growing rapidly; he had doubled the size of his garage and workshop by building a new shed on part of the orchard. Driving around the country, Frank was starting to see car and motorcycle workshops with petrol pumps outside. I need one of those, he thought.

Frank went to see Fred Manchett, who had two pumps at his Cambridge workshop.

"How do I get one of these pumps for my garage Fred"? Frank asked when he filled up his old van one day.

"I'll send the Shell rep over to see you," replied Fred. By November 1922, Frank Cartland had the first petrol pump in any Cambridgeshire village. He was the proud owner of a slim yellow and red Shell pump capped with a lit white shell globe.

"You are just like a child with a new toy". Margaret had laughed as she watched him tenderly polish its' glass casing.

Installing it had been backbreaking work. Joe, and even Spike, had tried to help to dig the large pit needed to take the petrol storage tank.

For a moment, having dug six feet down into the hard, chalky subsoil, and with his back aching and sweat pouring off him, Frank thought it would be good if John had been here to help. He hadn't thought about his dead brother in about a year.

In the January of that year, Margaret had discovered that she was pregnant again. She was delighted, Frank less so. Their first daughter Mary was a lively and healthy two-year old.

From the moment she could walk, Mary would find her way into the garage and was happy to be at her father's side playing with bits of his old engines and his spanners. Her hands were always oily and mucky.

"Don't encourage her," Margaret would often say. "I want her to grow up like a normal girl, not a dirty mechanic like you."

The birth of Mary had affected Frank greatly. Before her arrival there was little that had had any personal emotional impact on him. Apart that is from the surreal excitement he always felt when racing on the edge between disaster and success.

But his feelings for Mary were different. The love he felt for her was immediately strong - she was a part of him. Her happiness would always be the most important thing in his life, except when his racing passions got in the way.

Margaret was far from happy to witness Frank's continuing racing success.

"Even when you are here you're not at home," she said when he returned after another weekend away. "You are always in that bloody garage."

Frank had won another race and was proudly carrying a new silver trophy but this held no interest for her.

Margaret had always been a nervous girl, and now as a woman with a family, and with the worry of Frank's racing, every little thing seemed to cause her concern. She just couldn't understand Frank's passion for danger.

"Why can't he be like normal men and just go to the pub, get drunk and play cricket?" She would often moan to Frank's sister, Joan. Joan could only agree with her. She couldn't understand her young brother either.

"I'm afraid he's always been like it," she told Margaret. "I don't think he will change now."

Those words were not the ones Margaret wanted to hear.

When Frank first started race riding, Margaret had been supportive of his passion and had been happy to go with him to the race meetings. But with the early morning starts and the travel, often to bleak and cold and wet places, the novelty soon wore off.

She was much happier staying at home with her family. Their second daughter was born two weeks early, on a Saturday in September. She was delivered by Agnes Willes, as were all the other children in the village. The birth took place on another weekend that Frank was away racing. They called their new daughter Emily. She was a sickly child and kept Margaret awake most nights, giving her one more thing to worry about. When he was home Frank always seemed to be able to sleep through any noise.

"If there was an earthquake he wouldn't hear it," Margaret would often complain.

Frank was spending much more time away from home. He was travelling all over England to race his beloved motorbikes.

His first visit to the Isle of Man TT races had come in 1922,after he had rebuilt an engine for one of his best customers a local racer from Cambridge called Archie Jones.

"I've always wanted to race at the Isle of Man," Archie had said to Frank as he stood in Frank's workshop one day watching him rebuild an engine. "And it just so happens that I have managed to get an entry this year. I want you to run the bike for me."

Frank didn't need any persuading to take Archie's AJS motorbike to the famous racetrack.

"I have to go and help him, it's my job, and he's paying me," Frank said to an angry Margaret when he told her that he would be away for a week.

"Don't be surprised if I'm not here when you get back," Margaret replied. "The girls and I are going to stay with my parents."

Frank knew that the Fosters' would welcome their daughter and grandchildren with open arms, so that threat didn't worry him. Reginald Foster had never understood Frank. He had offered Frank the chance to join the family bakery business soon after the marriage and was shocked by Franks answer.

"Thanks' Mr. Foster (Frank never managed to call him Reginald) but I'm going to build my own motoring business. Can't imagine being a baker."

Frank and Archie happily set off early one misty June morning on the long road trip to Liverpool.

Standing at the front of the ferry as it slowly entered Douglas harbour, Frank could feel the excitement building inside him. One visit to the island and he was hooked. He became determined to race at the Isle of Man in 1923. Here he was surrounded by like-minded, passionate men, and a few women, he noticed. They had all travelled there for just one reason, to ride their motorbikes as fast as possible around this dangerous, difficult course.

Before the trial laps, Frank could see Archie Jones was very nervous. He spent more time in the latrines than the pits. Cautiously Archie went out on his first lap, but unfortunately, he was completely overwhelmed by his experience of the Isle of Man course. Much to Frank's disgust, Archie came into the pits after only three, slow practice laps. White faced, he took off his helmet.

"Sorry Frank, I think there's something wrong with the engine, it's not got much power."

"Alright, I'll have a look at it," said Frank without much enthusiasm.

What Frank really thought was … *the old bugger has scared himself silly.*

This was in fact the truth. Towards the end of his third lap, Archie had grown in confidence before arriving at Governor's Bridge at speed. The AJS had leapt into the air, and that split second of terror would live with Archie forever.

He thought he was going to die, but he just managed to keep control of the bucking bike and ride slowly back to the pits.

The pit area next to Frank and Archie was occupied by a real extrovert, a little guy called Freddie O'Hare.

Frank had been watching him all morning with great interest. Freddie was already well-known as a very quick motorcycle rider. He was always busy and covered in grease as he swore and worked all hours on his bikes.

He had a cigarette permanently clamped between his teeth. Jumping on his motorbike, he drove like the wind.

He's like an angry little wasp, thought Frank. This was just the sort of guy he could relate to.

Freddie was seven years older than Frank, and already a very experienced TT rider. He had first raced at the Isle of Man in 1912.

When Archie went off to change out of his leathers and go for another visit to the rest rooms, Frank boldly approached Freddie, who had just removed the carburetor from his bike.

"Would you mind trying out this AJS for me, Mr O'Hare?" said Frank.

"I'd really like to know what you think about my engine. The rider thinks it's no good."

Freddie looked up from his bike and, upon seeing the curly-haired, nervous looking young man standing next to him, said,

"What's your name, lad?"

"I…I'm Frank Cartland. It's my first time at the Isle of Man."

"Sure, I'd be happy to try out the bike, Frank. Let me finish putting the carb back on this piece of shit first."

"I … I thought you did a fast time this morning," said Frank, sounding a little surprised.

"Yeah, but I had to nearly bloody kill myself to do it. Herbert told me this engine would be one of his best, but it only got power at the top end. It's bloody near impossible to drive around this hell hole."

Frank knew that Herbert Wilson had been one of the top motorbike engine builders for the past five years. He also knew that Herbert's engines had won five TT races.

At that moment Frank wished he hadn't asked Freddie to try his engine.

Strapping on his helmet and pulling down his goggles, Freddie jumped on the AJS and roared off.

Archie arrived back to the pits just in time to see his motorbike disappear up the road in a cloud of grey dust.

"Hey, who the Hell's gone off on my bike?" he shouted to Frank.

"Ah ... that's Freddie O'Hare. He asked if he could try out the bike, he's thinking of getting an AJS," Frank lied.

"Oh, I suppose that's all right then," was all Archie said.

Three laps later, after lapping fast, almost as quick as on his own bike, Freddie came back into the pits.

"The bike's crap but the engine is fucking marvellous," said a grinning Freddie, as he pulled down his goggles.

"Frank, my boy, you can build a new engine for me anytime," he said as he put a greasy arm around Frank's shoulder.

After hearing Freddie's comments, a despondent Archie Jones said,

"Ok that's it for me, Frank. I'm not up to racing. I'm retiring today and from now on you can race my bike."

From that day forward, Freddie and Frank became firm friends. Freddie had seen in Frank a reflection of his younger self. Both men had left school early, without much education, had come from working-class families and had started rebuilding bicycles before progressing to motorcycles.

Freddie could see the same obsessive passion that he felt for racing reflected in young Frank's eyes.

For the next three racing seasons, Frank's engine-building reputation grew rapidly. Once Freddie O'Hare started winning races using Frank's engines, many more racers came knocking at Frank's workshop door. They were prepared to pay a high price for a Cartland-tuned engine.

The once peaceful, sleepy village of Burlham now often resounded to the sounds of high-revving motorcycles, upsetting the old locals and drowning out the birdsong. The Cartland motorcycle business was expanding fast.

11

Frank's first visit to the famous Brooklands track in Surrey was in 1923, when he raced alongside Freddie O'Hare. Frank was riding the AJS that still belonged to Archie Jones.

The scale of the place shocked him. Instead of the narrow roads he was used to racing along, Brooklands was a new world. Emerging from the tunnel under the track, Frank suddenly found himself in a vast amphitheatre, with the wide high banking filling his vision. His senses were hit by a strong scent of pine coming from the forest of trees on the banked area to his right. Then suddenly came the additional and familiar, intense smell, which was his favourite … the fumes of Castrol R drifting up from the paddock.

Venturing out onto the dirty-white concrete track, Frank quickly found that his bike wasn't suited to the high bumpy banking, although his bravery ensured that they were the tenth quickest after the practice period.
Forty noisy and smoky bikes roared out from the start in front of the Vickers sheds. Holding his tenth place for two laps, Frank had the twist grip throttle wide open when the AJS broke its chassis halfway around the Byfleet Banking. Fortunately, although it gave Frank a bit of a scare, he was able to bring the sparking bike to a safe stop, its chassis scraping the floor.

Racing on the fast Brooklands track had been a whole new exciting, overwhelming, experience for Frank.
"I just held the throttle wide open and turned into the Byfleet Banking. The AJS powered halfway up the slope and

we just sat there, all the way around flat out," he said
excitedly to Archie Jones as they pushed the broken bike
back into the paddock.
Archie just said.

"Rather you than me".
Frank, like George Marshall many years earlier, had fallen in
love with the whole Brooklands experience.
He excitedly explained this to Howard Jones when he got
back home.

"It's a complete contrast to the Isle of Man, but if you
just love speed it's brilliant," he said. "The wide track and
open banked turns suck you in, and it makes you want to go
faster and faster with every lap."
Overhearing this conversation from the next room,
Margaret ground her teeth together. She had grown to hate
the racing season. Between April and October, Frank was
away from home almost every weekend, and each time he
left she was never sure he would be coming back.

"Good of you to grace us with your presence," she
would say on the odd weekend he was at home.
Much to her dismay and Frank's delight, their daughter
Mary continued her interest in engines in preference to
dolls. She had become a real tomboy. Whenever Frank left
for a race there were tears and tantrums.

"Take me with you, take me with you," Mary would
say, clinging onto his leg.

At 5am one July morning, Frank and his mechanic Pete
were all ready to leave for a race meeting. Frank was
surprised that there was no sign of Mary; he had expected
the normal tears and protests at being left behind. Slightly

disappointed, he thought she must have stayed in bed this morning. He decided to look in and give her a kiss goodbye. But Mary was not in her bedroom. In some panic now, Frank rushed to wake up Margaret.

"Mary's not in her bed, I can't find her," he said. Growing frantic, with Margaret almost hysterical, they searched the house, the workshop and the garden sheds. Then Frank had an idea. He opened the back doors of the van where the motorbike and all the tools were securely stored away. Just as he thought, there was an extra passenger. Mary had taken blankets and a pillow from the house and made a cozy den for herself next to the bike.

"Come out of there this instant," shouted Margaret, who was angry and relieved.
Frank reached in and lifted his sobbing little girl out. Carrying her back to her bed he tucked her in and whispered in her ear,

"Promise I'll take you next time."
Frank did start to take Mary to some local race events. He thought that she would soon lose interest, but her interest just grew stronger. Hence Frank built her a little motorised bike.

"Not content with killing yourself, now you're going to kill my daughter," said an angry Margaret when she saw the machine.

"It will only go at 5mph, so she can't hurt herself," said Frank, once again trying to justify his actions to his hostile wife. Mary was delighted with her new toy.

"Oh, thank you, Daddy," she squealed, "now I'm going to be a racer just like you."

Her mother just rolled her eyes and turned away, feeling helpless. Mary was soon chugging around the village upsetting the elderly locals.

Frank had become obsessed with winning an Isle of Man TT race. He couldn't afford to race there until 1925, and then it was on an old bike belonging to Freddie O'Hare. Frank entered it for the Junior TT. The previous year Freddie had used the bike to win the race, but it was already a year old. Now that it was out of date, Frank struggled to keep up with the newer bikes. After practice he was a little despondent to be only the fifteenth quickest.

"Cheer up, Frank," Freddie said. "I'll take you for a drink tonight, that'll take your mind off it."
It was then, thanks to Freddie, that Frank was introduced to some of the other pleasures that the Isle of Man had on offer for the riders. Each year Freddie stayed at the Metropole Hotel in Ramsey. The hotel manager reserved a room for him. It was room 8 - his lucky number. There were several girls on the island who "collected" famous riders, but Freddie had had a regular partner Hazel Compton for a few years. She would always spend the nights of TT week with Freddie and be in the winner's circle waiting to share his glory and champagne after the race.

Before practice in 1925, Freddie had introduced Frank to Hazel.
"Is he going to be as famous as you?" Hazel asked Freddie after Frank had gone off to work on his bike. "If he is then my friend Susan would like to meet him."

"Of course he bloody is, he's a quick lad," said Freddie.

"Let's fix them up for tonight," came the reply.

That evening Frank found himself at dinner sitting opposite a pretty, freckled brunette called Susan Nolan. When Freddie had told him earlier that evening that he had someone he wanted Frank to meet, Frank had assumed it would be another racing guy. He certainly wasn't expecting this attractive young woman that he now had sitting opposite him.

After a few too many beers they were all in a very relaxed mood.

Walking back along the seafront, Susan put her arm around Frank, who instinctively bent down and kissed her.

"Are we going back to your room?" asked Susan.

"Looks like we are," Frank replied.

Freddie had booked Frank into the Metropole in the room next to him. Frank soon found that Susan was a very willing and experienced partner. The walls of the hotel were thin, and they could hear the moans and creaking bed from Freddie and Hazel's activity next door.

This made them even more aroused Frank not getting off to sleep until 3am.

He had asked for an alarm call at 6am and when it came he felt terrible. He had a splitting headache and was aware that he had to be ready to start the race at 9am. He was not at all happy.

Beside him, Susan was sobbing.

"What's the matter with you?" said Frank. "Are you sorry you stayed?"

"No... it's not that," she said, sniffing. "I'm just worried about what's going to happen to you today."

"I'll be fine," said Frank, "why would you worry about me?"

"Well, last year I spent the night in this same room with Johnny Halliday, and he was killed the next day. And the year before Robert ..."

"Get dressed and bugger off out of here," a very angry Frank interrupted. The scar on his forehead was glowing pink.

Crying, Susan gathered up her clothes and did just that. Unlike most of his racing mates, Frank rarely swore. But now he was very angry. Not with that stupid girl, but with himself. He had let himself down. He had come to the Isle of Man to race his bike, not to sleep with a local good-time girl. *I've let my cock rule my head again*, he thought.

The race didn't prove a success for Frank. Although he finished without any real incident, he was down in tenth place. He knew he had been too careful and too slow. He swore he wouldn't let it happen again. In future years he wouldn't drink before a race and would always ensure that he slept alone.

Frank had decided not to race at all in 1926. He was determined to save all his money so he could afford to buy a motorbike that was good enough to win the Isle of Man Senior TT in 1927.

When he told Margaret that he wouldn't be racing the following year she didn't give him a chance to inform her of his reason.

"Good, it's about time you grew up and stopped playing these stupid, dangerous games," she said. "You will have plenty to do here; the house needs painting, the fence is falling down and the trees in the orchard need pruning, just for a start. Then you can spend some weekend time with me and the girls for a change."

Once again, things did not all turn out as Margaret had hoped.

Frank was very busy building engines and looking after his racing customers, so he was still away many weekends. Also, because of Freddie O'Hare, he did manage to visit a racetrack that he had been avidly reading about in his motoring magazines. It would make a lasting impression on him.

Spa-Francorchamps in Belgium was the circuit.

"Frank, I really could do with your bloody help next week," Freddie had said when he called at the garage. He had arrived to pick up the new engine Frank had just finished building for Freddie's TT Norton motorbike.

"I'm racing my sidecar outfit next weekend and my stupid passenger has broken his bloody leg. Would you do me a favour and stand in for him?"

"Sure thing, course I will," said Frank without a second thought.

"Great, pick you up Tuesday morning about 6, we're catching the lunchtime ferry from Felixstowe."

"Felixstowe?" said Frank. "Where are we going?"

"Spa, of course," said Freddie as he jumped into his Austin van. "Make sure you bring your passport," he shouted out of the window as he left.

"What do you mean you're going to Belgium next week?" said a seething Margaret. "I told the girls we would take them to the seaside at Clacton."

"Sorry, but I can't let Freddie down, he needs me," said Frank weakly. It was a rather unfortunate response. Now, almost screaming at him, Margaret said,

"I really don't understand you at all, you bloody stupid fool. You can let your family down but not that horrible little man."

The strained atmosphere in the Cartland household was made even worse on Sunday. Charlie Willis called in to see them for a cup of tea.

"I hear you are off to Belgium next week, Frank," he said. Charlie had been horse racing in Belgium many times and ridden a lot of winners over there before the war.

"Belgium's a great country, you'll love it," Charlie continued. "The locals are all very friendly, I'll give you the address of a friend of mine in Brussels."
Frank gave him a quick kick under the table to shut him up. Margaret sat stony-faced and silent.

On the Monday evening, Margaret had taken their girls back to her parents' bakery once again. Without saying goodbye she left him alone in Ivy Cottage.
It was with great relief that Frank got into Freddie's van early on Tuesday morning, and together they trundled happily off to Felixstowe. His family problems were soon forgotten.
The ferry crossing was thankfully smooth, and by late-afternoon they found themselves driving on the long, straight road leading to Brussels.

It was almost dark when Freddie said,

"Let's stop here for the night."

They could see the lights of a village ahead, and there was a small building with a petrol pump outside, which looked remarkably like Frank's own garage. As they pulled up outside the garage, a skinny young lad came out to meet them.

"DO YOU SPEAK ENGLISH?" said Freddie in a slow and loud voice.

"No need to shout at the poor boy," Frank said. He was about to try some of his pigeon French.

The lad continued.

"Oui ... I do ... petit ... a little, me Robart Virrea, welcome…Mr. O'Hare."

"Could we stay here tonight?" said Frank. With the help of hand-signs they made the lad understand and they were invited into his home. Inside, his father greeted them like long-lost brothers, shaking hands and hugging both. Robart had disappeared into another room. He came back with a pile of motorcycle magazines, proudly opening one to show a grainy picture of Freddie. He was in his oily overalls, had a fag in his mouth, and was carrying the TT Silver Trophy.

"Please, Mr. O'Hare, will sign for me?" said Robart. Freddie, of course, was delighted to be the centre of attention. Next morning, after a large breakfast, they continued their merry way to Spa.

They arrived at Spa before they realised they were there. Driving onto the road at La Source hairpin, and down the hill, they suddenly found they were already on the race circuit.

Leaving the trailer and bike in the paddock with a couple of the other English riders who had recently arrived, Freddie and Frank went for a drive around the 14km circuit.

It wasn't long before they understood what a very fast and dangerous track Spa Francorchamps was.

"Bugger me, it's going to be flat out for most of the lap," said Freddie.

"It's so narrow that you can reach out and touch the houses and trees," said a slightly worried Frank.

"For Christ's sake, don't do that," said Freddie. "You won't have much to do, just lean right over the back of the bike at the three hairpins, the rest of the time just stay flat down in the sidecar out of the air stream."

Frank looked doubtful.

After having being given a bed by their new Brussels friends, the pair spent the following night sleeping in the back of the van. Frank didn't sleep much. For the first time in his life he felt slightly scared.

Practice day went well. Freddie rode sensibly as he learnt his way around the long track. Frank, although not entirely happy having someone else in control of his destiny, started to enjoy the experience. He learnt quickly how to move around the sidecar to balance the bike on the corners and bends. Freddie was the one person he did trust with his life. As practice ended, they were fifth fastest and quite satisfied with their efforts.

That evening they enjoyed a few beers in the bar of Le Relais de Pommard, a hotel next to the circuit. Two other English riders were there, Jimmy Smart and his sidecar passenger, Peter Houge. They had qualified third in the practice session.

This pair had been the most successful British sidecar partnership for the past three seasons, and they had won the Isle of Man sidecar TT the previous year.

"Better watch your bloody back tomorrow, Jimmy, I'll be coming for you in the race," joked Freddie.

"You won't see me for dust, old mate," said Jimmy. Have another beer and shut up."

Peter had been the sidecar passenger for Jimmy for the last four seasons, and Frank was keen to get some tips about the best way to balance the bike through the very fast Masta Kink.

"I almost smashed my head against the house on the left there this morning," said Frank.

"Yeah, it's pretty hairy, isn't it? We're doing over a ton through there, keep your head down," said a sullen Peter.

"Thanks, but I'd already decided to do that," said Frank sarcastically.

"Sorry, Frank, but there's not much more I can say. It's just instinct really. Follow the bends and lean into them. You're like me, here because you need the buzz." After a short pause he added.

"Sometimes I wish I didn't. This place scares me".

"Me too," said Frank. "I'll get you another drink."

Like Frank, Peter had a wife and two young children back home in England.

"I've decided this will be my last race," he said. "My wife's been nagging me to stop…I'll be thirty-five next week. The kids are eight and ten and I've not seen much of them growing up over the past four years.

Been lucky so far, but going to pack this mad game in. Haven't told Jimmy yet, so keep it to yourself."

"Course I will," said Frank.

Both remained silent and sipped their drinks, thinking about the risks they would be facing in the morning.

Race day dawned overcast and cool, but in this region of the Ardennes, the weather was always extremely unpredictable. The sidecar race was run over ten laps and began in dry conditions at one pm. There had already been two races for singles: A Senior 350cc and a Junior 250cc.

The atmosphere was tense before the start of the sidecar race. A popular local Belgian rider had gone off the road on the straight before Stavelot, when his engine had sized, and news that he been killed came through to the paddock just as the sidecar outfits were preparing to go out for their race.

The conflicting emotions running through Frank's head were extreme. He was looking forward to the challenge of this great track, but he knew his future remained in the hands of Freddie already fired up for the race. Frank didn't like this feeling of not being in control.

"Okay, Fearless, let's bloody do this, see you on the other side," Freddie said, shaking Frank's hand.

Frank's mouth was dry, but he managed to say:

"Yeah ... let's do it."

At that moment, he wished he were back home, or anywhere but here. They strapped on their helmets and pulled down their goggles.

There were twenty sidecar outfits on the grid and the pervasive noise, smells and smoke invaded all of Frank's senses as the engine revs rose to a crescendo.

All the riders were straining, holding the engines against the brakes, until the drop of the Belgium flag released the mass of screaming, swarming, swerving sidecars.

The race started very well for them. By lap four of the ten-lap race, Freddie's Douglas bike was going well in a comfortable fourth place, only six seconds behind Jimmy and Peter.

Freddie was getting more confident each lap. Now flat out through the daunting Masta Kink, Frank became aware that he was smiling. Much to his surprise, he was enjoying himself.

They were closing the gap to Jimmy, and as they came down the hill and passed the pits to start their final lap, Frank could clearly see his HRD outfit. It was only two seconds ahead at the 11 km mark, and they were gaining with every yard. Frank edged Freddie on.

As they approached the fast-left-hand bend at Blanchimont, Frank noticed Peter glance back and urgently give a slowdown signal. Freddie instantly relaxed his throttle hand and the bike slowed, but they were still travelling fast as they rounded the bend to find that the track was very wet.

A sudden localized shower had rendered the track glass-like. The Douglas slid sideways as Freddie frantically fought for control. Frank instinctively moved his weight over the sliding rear wheel and somehow Freddie managed to keep the unit on the road. In a flash they were through and continued quickly down through the left-hand curve and onto La Source hairpin.

Accelerating out of La Source, they were greeted by the chequered flag to end the race.

Most of the Spa circuit was still dry as they went out on their slowing-down lap. Freddie grinned at Frank and slapped him on the shoulder. Frank grinned back and gave him the thumbs up sign. Both were happy to have finished in a good position, although they were not sure what that position was.

When they reached the Blanchimont turn it had stopped raining and a weak yellow sun appeared. The low, grey clouds, cast faint long shadows from the people and the ambulance, which was blocking the track.

"Stop the bike, Freddie. Let's find out what's happened," shouted Frank.

Freddie slid the bike to a stop. They left their bike and ran to the edge of the track. Here a six-foot high thorn hedge bordered a ten-foot wide strip of grass. Frank's nose picked up his favorite smell of fresh cut grass. Then he noticed the deep grooves in the grass leading to a large hole in the hedge.

"I don't like the look of this," said Freddie as they walked towards the hole. Looking over the hedge, Frank replied,

"Christ! There's a twenty-foot drop down here."

Way below them they could see a group of people gathered around the twisted remains of Jimmy Smart's HRD motorbike. Frank could just make out the number nine - Jimmy's lucky number. Others were lifting a lifeless body onto a stretcher.

"Look...over there, it's Jimmy," said Freddie, pointing to the left. They watched their friend hobbling slowly away from the scene.

"Then that must be Peter on the stretcher," said Frank quietly.

They walked back to the Douglas and Freddie automatically drove back to the pits. The news from the deeply-distressed Jimmy was the worst.

"There was no warning," he explained. "One second it was dry, next the track was like a skating rink ... there was nothing I could do."
When the bike had gone through the hedge and hurled down the drop, Jimmy and Peter had been thrown in different directions. Jimmy was the lucky one, bouncing across the moss and pine floor, somehow missing all the fir trees. The soft moss had cushioned his fall, and with relief he got up. He was bruised but largely uninjured. Dusting himself down he went to find Peter. Jimmy found him lying face down in the Eau Rouge stream, which ran alongside and under the Spa circuit.

"There was no blood, nothing. I...I thought he had just been knocked out. Then when I pulled him out, his neck ..." Jimmy broke down completely. It was obvious that Peter's luck had finally run out.
His descent had been abruptly halted as his body slammed into the large trunk of a Belgian fir tree. Death was instant, his neck broken.

There were no celebrations that evening at Spa. The third-place trophies Freddie and Frank had won were left discarded in the back of the van. Arrangements had to be made for Peter's body to be returned to England. Frank and Freddie stayed on to help Jimmy with the harrowing task. Frank had sent a telegram home to let the family know he was fine, but that he needed to stay in Belgium an extra day. He didn't give a reason.

The following afternoon the body of Peter Hough was given a somber civic send off from Spa station. His flower bedecked coffin was placed on the 3pm train to begin his last journey, back home to Manchester. As they watched the steam train move slowly out of Spa station, Frank said,

"You realise that the last thing Peter did was to warn us?"

"Yeah, I know, bloody good bloke," said Freddie. Freddie and Frank spent most of their trip home in silence. They didn't stop at Brussels as planned, as they were impatient to catch the next ferry. Both were reflecting on the events at Spa. Freddie broke the silence.

"Fucking place," he said. "I'm never going to race there again."

Frank said nothing. He had been thinking just how much he had been enjoying the race until that fatal moment. Now he felt guilty ... he knew that despite Peter's death he would go back and race at Spa. If he ever had the chance.

He also knew that Freddie would too. This guy had won races at the most dangerous track in the world, the Isle of Man.

With his nature, Freddie would soon recover from this shock and would be looking forward to his next trip to Spa Francorchamps.

Frank said little of his Belgium trip when he got home. He was trying to keep the death of Peter Hough from his family. It was unfortunate that the motorcycle press called to interview him on the Wednesday after the event, so Margaret and Joan soon found out.

"That could have been you, riding with that madman O'Hare," Margaret shouted at him

"Well, that was my first and last sidecar race," said Frank, and he meant it. He really had no intention of repeating the experience. From now on when he raced he would be in control of his own fate.

The following month he went to the Isle of Man just to look after Freddie O'Hare's motorbike, but he was still determined to be driving there the following year.

SENIOR
Tourist Trophy Race
Friday, June 17th, 1927.

OFFICIAL PROGRAMME.
Organised by
THE AUTO-CYCLE UNION

12

For the 1927 race, Frank had spent all his, and his family's money amounting to £95 on a new Norton racing motorbike. When she found out Margaret's distress was obvious.

"How could you be so irresponsible?" she complained when he turned up with the gleaming new, black racing motorbike. "You have a family to support."
With the silver and black petrol tank proudly displaying the Norton name on both of its sides, Frank had been excited and keen to show off his new pride and joy. Now he had to defend himself once again.

"It will be worth it when I win," he said, trying to justify the cost to himself as much as to Margaret. "We will get even more customers, and I will be able to sell the Norton for a profit."

"We never see you now as it is, so how will more customers help that? You're a selfish bastard," she said before storming out of the workshop and slamming the door. Frank hadn't had time to answer. He was angry. *Why does this woman always make me feel so guilty?* he asked himself. *She tries to take away all my pleasure.*

The Norton CS1 bike, with its single cylinder overhead cam engine, was a new design developed especially for the TT races of 1927.
This bike is the most beautiful thing I've seen since the old Triumph that Howard Jones arrived on back in 1913, he thought with a grin.

Frank and Peter Betts left Burlham at 4am that June morning, once again starting the long journey north for Liverpool, where the ferry that would take them to the Isle of Man waited. Frank was full of confidence and happy as he steadily drove the Morris van, with the Norton carefully strapped into the space behind him and his young mechanic Pete at his side. This was going to be his year. Mary had woken up to give him a good luck kiss.

"I know you are going to win, Daddy. I will pray for you at church on Sunday". She'd whispered.
Margaret had stayed in bed, pretending to sleep. She wouldn't even say goodbye.

Once more Frank stood at the front of the old ferry, watching as the captain slowly maneuvered it into the dock at Douglas harbour. Frank knew the next few days would be the most important of his life.

The Senior Tourist Trophy was always the most prestigious motorcycle race of the season. All the top riders from the UK and Europe had travelled to the Isle of Man to win it. At 7am on a misty Tuesday morning, each rider presented themselves and their bikes for scrutiny. Frank was allocated the number 51 for the event. With shock he remembered that his father had been 51 when he died. It was the day Frank's real life had begun. He felt that must be a good omen.
Practice started the following morning, at 6am on 15th June. The day dawned dry and cool, with a light mist over the mountain section of the course. For practice, the Isle of Man roads were still open to normal traffic.

One of Frank's rivals, Archie Wright, also riding a new Norton, approached Kirk Michael very fast and was forced to brake hard to avoid a local delivery van moving slowly in the middle of the road.

Poor Archie lost control of the bike and was thrown off, sliding head first into a flint wall. The undamaged bike slid down the road. Archie was killed instantly, his neck broken on impact with the solid wall.

Frank arrived on the scene only twenty seconds after the accident and clearly saw Archie's broken body as he slowly rode past. He immediately closed his mind and focused on the narrow road ahead.

Then he remembered what Freddie had once said to him.

"When I see something bad I twist the throttle wide open and go as fast as possible. Because I know most of the other guys slow down when they see a bad accident."

At the time, Frank had thought that was wrong and uncaring. Now he realised that for him, winning was all that mattered, and at any cost.

Every rider knew that death at the Isle of Man was part of the great risk. Each time they ventured out onto the 37 miles of public roads that made up the course, there was a chance they would never come back.

Narrow roads, stone walls, lampposts and a steep drop off the side of the mountain sections were just some of the hazards they faced.

It was an accepted part of the "ride for glory" for these men, who were only really alive when risking all.

Frank was very happy with the sleek black Norton, without taking too many risks he managed 3rd fastest in practice. It was his first ride on the bike and he was quicker than his great mate, Freddie O'Hare, who for the 1927 race was riding a HRD machine.

The commentators made a big thing of the rivalry between them.

"Here come Flying Freddie and Fearless Frank, who's going to be the quickest on this lap?" became a common announcement.

"Bloody hell, Fearless, looks like I'm going to have to get my finger out to beat you this year," said Freddie to Frank after practice.

"It's time you made way for us youngsters," Frank joked, knowing that Freddie was becoming sensitive about his age.

Frank slept well the night before the race and when start time came he was in an optimistic mood. Confident that he could win the famous silver trophy, he knew that he could ride some of the corners faster than he had in practice. Frank's start time arrived. He pulled on his brown leather helmet and adjusted his goggles.

"Good luck, Frank," his mechanic Pete said as he slapped him on the back.

Now he was completely alone. He stood in silence, waiting, his hands tightly clutching the black rubber grips on the drop handlebars of his precious Norton. Looking forward at the wide expanse of empty road ahead of him, he was calm, and his mind was clear. He was ready.

Stopwatch in hand, the starter raised then dropped his flag. At last! ... Frank accelerated away on the most important ride of his life.

The Senior TT was over 7 laps of the 37-mile course. By lap5, after racing for more than three hours, Frank stormed into his pit for his last petrol re-fuelling stop.

"You are only five seconds behind Alec Bennett who is leading," his mechanic Peter Betts shouted in his ear.

"Freddie is at least ten seconds behind you."
Frank accepted the clean pair of goggles Pete handed him. He was relieved to be able to see clearly again. The old goggles were covered with dead flies and streaks of engine grease. With the buildup of dust and oil, his face had become a dirty black mask.

"No problem, I'm going to win this race," Frank shouted back to Pete as he slammed the petrol cap shut and roared off again. He was confident there were a couple of corners that he could take even quicker to make up that amount of time. Frank tucked his body down low over the petrol tank and wound the throttle flat out. Down the hill to Kirk Michael Corner, he went through faster than ever before, smiling to himself as he brushed the left-hand verge. This was 15 miles round the final lap.
I'm nearly half way he thought, I can really do this.
Powerfully out of Ramsey Hairpin, his self-built engine was running beautifully. It was just touching the flint wall on the inside of the bend as he leant the bike in, climbing up Snaefell, the 30-mile marker.

With the engine screaming flat out through the sweeping curves of Bungalow and Windy Corners, Frank was in the zone, completely at one with his cherished Norton. For a second, he allowed himself to dream of victory…he could even picture the Hermes, winged silver trophy.

With only two miles to go, on the descent to Creg-ny-Baa, Frank took the right-hand bend fractionally too fast. He instantly knew that he was in trouble. The Norton ran a few inches wide, off line by just three inches. But this was the difference between glory and disaster.

Frank's beloved motorbike slid onto the loose gravel at the edge of the road, he was riding on instinct. Fighting desperately for control, for a split second he felt relief as he thought he had saved it, but then the rear wheel slipped off the edge of the road. His wonderful dream had turned into his worst nightmare.

The violent movement of the bike sent Frank flying down the 40-foot drop in a graceful arc. Halfway down the mountainside his body hit, right knee first, against a large, grey granite boulder, the impact ripping his racing leathers open as they were caught on the jagged rock.

Fortunately, this slowed his progress a little, but his kneecap had been shattered against the unyielding ancient hard rock.

137

Years later, Frank would clearly remember that moment every time he tapped and broke the shell of his boiled egg at breakfast. A deep gulley eventually arrested his free fall partway down the steep slope. On impact his right leg folded under him and snapped like a broken twig.

Instantly looking up he saw his Norton fly over him, just a foot above his head. With a sickening crunching scream, it slammed into another large, granite outcrop. With a final loud hiss, like a dying man's last breath, the poor Norton's remains came to a smoking, steaming halt.

Then the pain kicked in and Frank Cartland passed out.

13

The Moncrieff's wealth had been accumulated in the cotton mills of Lancashire. Simon Moncrieff was the third-generation owner of Moncrieff's Mills in Preston. Simon, approaching fifty years old, had been a widower for five years when Alice Morris seduced him with her charm and beauty.

Alice, only twenty-one when they first met, knew the effect her beauty had on men and she fully intended to use all her charms. The Morris family worked as shopkeepers, with Alice's father and his brother running two shops close to Moncrieff's Mills. Much of their custom being generated from the mill workers.

Alice knew exactly what she wanted out of life and she had no intention of spending her life stuck in Preston.

She needed a rich husband, widower Simon Moncrieff was her target and she made sure that he noticed her from his carriage, as it passed her fathers' shop, on his many visits to his mills.

Despite his family's protests, Simon quickly became besotted with Alice Morris and she soon snared her man. The couple were married at St Stephen Church in Warrington on 20th August 1900.

Simon had two sons from his first marriage. Both were now in their twenties, just a few years older than his new wife. They saw Alice exactly for what she was - a gold digger - and they hated her. To placate the boys, Simon handed over the control of the family mills to them, leaving him free to attempt to keep his new, young wife contented.

With Alice's pressure Simon purchased a large old manor house in Cheshire and their lavish parties soon becoming famed throughout the county.

Both Simon and Alice were delighted when their daughter Silvia was born in 1902. From the moment of her birth, Alice had just one ambition for her daughter. This was to marry her into a titled old English family.

With no cotton mills to worry him, gambling became Simon Moncrieff's' only real passion in life. Alice soon realised this would be an excellent opportunity for her to forward her ambitions for Silvia. With encouragement from Alice, Simon took up membership with some of the best London gentleman's clubs.

It was in the Mayfair Club, while playing roulette, that he was first introduced to Lord John Marshall, a fellow hardened gambler.

It had not been a chance meeting. Alice had arranged for the Honourable Richard Mears, one of her London lovers, to bring the two men together.

The war had rather stalled her ambitions, but to Alice's delight, the Moncrieff family received an invite to the Marshall box at the 1919 Epsom Derby. It was the first Derby since the war, and an enormous crowd had gathered on Epsom Downs.

Both John Marshall and Simon Moncrieff had large bets on the race, with Lord Marshall placing £100 on the horse of his friend Lord Derby, and Simon Moncrieff placing £100 on a horse called Grand Parade, which had been trained in Ireland. He had seen the horse winning a good race the previous year. Grand Parade was the outsider.

"Your horse has no chance, he has been injured, didn't you know?" said John Marshall to Simon smugly, as the horses lined up behind the starting tapes. Grand Parade won The Derby, at 33:1, winning Simon Moncrieff £3,300.

"He doesn't need the bloody money," said a disgusted John Marshall to his wife as he tore up his losing ticket.

"Thank you for the invite John. It has been a very enjoyable day. I will buy you all dinner and champagne tonight" Simon said to John Marshall as they left the track.

"Should think you bloody will" muttered Lord Marshall in response.

It was at Epsom that George and Silvia met for the first time. Now aged seventeen, Silvia had become a very attractive and spirited young lady. At 5 feet 7 inches tall, with long, silk-like, raven-black hair and dark-brown eyes. It was fair to say that her looks were stunning. She had inherited the seduction skills of her mother, and George was immediately under her spell.

Alice had already turned her daughter into an experienced young woman, having encouraged one of her own lovers to seduce Silvia and take her virginity when she was just sixteen. The following day Silvia had said,

"Thank you, Mother," and smiling, added, "I'm glad that's out of the way, you can have him back now."

Alice had primed Silvia before the meeting at Epsom, making sure that she encouraged any interest from George – something that Silvia was very happy to do.

"What do you think of him?" said Alice when they were alone watching the horse's parade in the paddock.

"Rather disappointing to look at, but I'm sure I can turn him into something presentable," said Silvia with a confident smile.

The mothers of both families were happy. George's obvious interest in Silvia delighted Victoria Marshall, and this development was exactly as she had planned it.

Victoria saw marriage into the Moncrieff family, with the vast fortune she knew that Silvia would eventually inherit, as the best chance to ensure financial security for the Marshall dynasty. And, judging by seventy-year-old Simon Moncrieff's aged appearance; she reckoned that the inheritance would come very soon.

The following year, 1920, saw the re-opening of Brooklands race course. Both George and Silvia attended this first race meeting with their respective parents. George, of course, had been there once before.

"I'll show you around if you like," he said to Silvia.

"Thank you, George that would be lovely," Silvia replied.

To George's delight, he found Silvia very attentive, and was amazed that she was also passionate about racing cars.

"I'm going to race cars here as soon as I get my money," he excitedly told her. "My grandfather left me £5000, which will be available when I reach twenty-one."

"If you marry me we could get a racing car together, and much sooner than that," Silvia replied. Her comment left George in a state of shock.

"I ... I would really like that, but I will have to ask mother first," he replied.

Inwardly, Silvia groaned and thought what a pathetic young man George was. But his obvious weakness also pleased her. She was excited by the prospect of the amount of power she could soon hold. Once married to her, George would be putty in her hands.

Simon, and especially Alice Moncrieff, were very happy for the relationship to develop, as marrying into the old Marshall family would be the fulfillment of her dreams.

On the return to Sefton Manor from the trip to Brooklands, George found his mother alone in the drawing room.

"Mother," he said nervously, "I have decided that I would like to get married."

Victoria was, of course, expecting this conversation. She and Alice Moncrieff had already agreed that it would be a satisfactory arrangement for both families.

"Who is the young lady? I hope she is from a good family?" said Victoria, feigning surprise.

"It…it's Silvia Moncrieff, the girl who was at Brooklands," stammered George.

"She is certainly very pretty; I will have to discuss it with your father when he comes back from London."

Victoria was delighted. Silvia Moncrieff's money would do very well.

She put George out of his misery two days later. He had been moping around the manor and looking at her expectantly every time she walked into the room.

"Very well, George, you have our blessing. You may ask Silvia Moncrieff to marry you,".

"Tha … thank you, Mother," said a delighted George. He went across the room and tried to give his mother a hug. Victoria immediately stepped away…as if her son had some infectious disease.

George proposed to Silvia on Christmas Eve 1920 as the two families met for drinks at The Ritz. An anxious and slightly drunk George, later in the evening, managed to get Silvia alone.

"I…I would like to marry you Silva… If you will have me".

"This is my answer George" she said putting her arms around him and kissing him passionately on the lips.

They married in April 1921, all members of both families were happy…for a short while at least.
The marriage, a lavish affair, was. held at Sefton Manor. Alice Moncrieff, still a very beautiful woman, and wanting to demonstrate her new position in society, had invited more than one hundred of her northern family and friends to the wedding, much to the dismay of Victoria Marshall.

"They are all so uncouth," she said to Lady Roseberry, one of her guests. "I cannot understand a word most of them are saying."They may as well be talking in a foreign language."
The contrast with the 'old' families that had been invited by the Marshalls was striking.
Simon Moncrieff was now rather a pathetic figure. At seventy-two his health had suffered markedly over the previous two years. Gout and arthritis were giving him great pain. During the wedding the official photographer asked,

"Please come over here, sir, and stand next to your beautiful granddaughter."
Alice had found this extremely amusing.
The newlywed's first night together was a real delight for George. Certainly, it was one of the most pleasant experiences of his life so far.

His father had surprised him at the wedding reception by handing him a book. It had a worn, red leather cover with the words Kama Sutra embossed in faded and flaking gold letters.

"This little book was given to me by my uncle when I was your age," Lord Marshall explained. "It has served me very well, look after it."

After a short awkward silence, he shook George's hand, turned and went back to his drinking cronies. Those were the most words his father had ever said to George.

Since his early traumatic experience with his brothers, sex was something that made George very nervous, and boarding school had confused him even more. Several boys experimented on each other. George was always too afraid to join in.

Silvia, on the other hand, knew exactly what to do, and soon took him in hand. She read the Kama Sutra with great enthusiasm.

"How wonderful of your father to give us this book I think it's the best wedding present we've had," she said. "I'll have to thank him myself."

George wasn't sure if she was joking.

Silvia soon had George experimenting with many of the more unusual positions described in the book, but unfortunately his lack of fitness and stamina often left her frustrated.

The Marshall and Moncrieff families were delighted when Silvia fell pregnant only six months after the wedding. George and Silvia had set up home at the Lodge House, in the grounds of the manor. With three stories, five bedrooms and castellated roof, it was certainly large enough for them.

This will do until I get my hands on that old manor, thought Silvia.

On 3rd June 1922, their first child was born; a healthy boy whom they named William John Marshall. It was with great relief when Silvia noticed that baby William looked much more like her than George, although he did have the Marshall blond hair.

Simon Moncrieff, with substantial pressure from his wife, and considerable envy from Victoria Marshall, had been buying all the latest, top-class motor cars.

Silvia, having been well taught by her mother, used her charm on her father and said,

"All our friends have Bentleys now, Daddy, don't you think it's about time George and I had one? It would be the best present ever."

After a full week of constant requests from his daughter he gave in.

"Very well, my girl," he said. "I'll leave you to choose the best model for your growing family."

Just three days later, Silvia drove back to Sefton Lodge, shattering the peace of the country estate with the bellowing exhaust note of a 1923 dark green racing Bentley.

Knowing Silvia was out Victoria Marshall had been at the lodge for an hour advising George that he should more take control of his wayward wife.

"You really must take charge," she scolded. "You let her do whatever she wants. Her place is at home looking after you and our grandson William."

George was silent under his mother's nagging, but wished he had the strength to tell her what he was thinking, which was … *you didn't look after me when I was growing up*.

At that moment, Silvia arrived home. George and his mother hurried outside to see what was causing all the noise.

Ignoring her mother-in-law Silvia said.

"Jump in, Georgie,", as she slid the large machine to a stop, "we are going to take this old thing to Brooklands." George jumped into the passenger seat and, in a shower of gravel, Silvia roared away. The privileged young couples were off to turn their Brooklands dreams into reality, while an open-mouthed and angry Victoria Marshall could only watch in despair.

14

George was happy to win a few of the small handicap races at Brooklands. But much to his discomfort, Silvia, although not allowed to race, was able to lap the great concrete bowl faster than he could when she tested their Bentley.

With the money Simon Moncrieff had been paying him for road cars, and the fact that George wasn't a bad driver, W. O. Bentley invited George to join the Bentley team at the 1925 Le Mans 24-hour race as a reserve driver. For that honour, Mr. Bentley charged George £500 to cover all their expenses.
Silvia went with George, leaving their two-year-old William at the lodge with his nanny.

Les Vingt-Quatre Heures Du Mans was first run in May 1923, when a Bentley finished 5th. They had entered just one car for 1924 and won the race. A confident W.O. Bentley entered four cars in 1925, hoping to ensure another victory. Catching the ferry at Dover and landing in Calais, George and Silvia started the drive down through northern France in their touring Bentley. All the Bentley drivers had planned an overnight stop at the Hotel Le Maurice in Paris to start their Le Mans adventure. After a champagne fueled dinner, the whole party went next door to the Revue Bar, which was considered the most outrageous club in Paris. Star performer was an exotic dancer, Hellen Dupery, whose lithe, barely-clothed body, cropped blond hair and wide smile captivated all who saw her.
Especially George Marshall.

"My, Georgie, I've not seen you this excited since our wedding night," Silvia whispered to him with amusement.

"I … I just think she is a lovely dancer," said a red-faced George. Silvia was delighted to see him so animated. Maybe this will make him more interesting in bed tonight, she thought. Hellen was invited back to the Bentley table after her performance and, much to the surprise and delight of all, she told them she would also be at Le Mans for the race.

"I plan to race there myself very soon," Hellen announced.

"So, do I," said Silvia excitedly. "We should race there together." Everyone thought this was a splendid idea …everyone except George.

Returning from the Revue Bar around 2am, they went straight to bed. While they lay in the single beds in their Paris hotel room, an intoxicated George slurred,

"I think you will find women are not allowed to drive in the Le Mans 24-hour race. You need stamina and strength to handle a racing car for that length of time." Silvia said nothing; she just clenched her jaw as she always did when angry. *I'll show you, Georgie Porgy*, she thought. An excess of champagne made sure George wasn't fit to put up any sort of performance that night.

Silvia lay in bed frustrated and unable to sleep. She already loved this new, exciting race, and she hadn't even seen the racetrack yet. She also loved the dashing, worldly Bentley team drivers. Now, finding a likeminded strong-willed woman like Hellen, it all seemed so perfect. Silvia was growing very tired of George, who never seemed to have any confidence and was still afraid to upset his mother.

The "Bentley Boys" were all wealthy, experienced racing drivers. They were worldly men full of confidence and she knew that they were all mesmerised by her style and beauty. Seducing one of these boys will be child's play, she thought, becoming aroused at the very idea.

She looked over at George and sighed. He already had his mouth open and was snoring lightly. She would be pleasuring herself to sleep again tonight.

Dawn on practice day arrived, spreading a light yellow glow across the Marshall's bedroom. Knowing he would be driving fast laps on this difficult and dangerous Le Mans track, George had woken around 3am and had not been able to get back to sleep.

About 7am, Silvia heard him being sick in the bathroom next to their room.

"What's the matter, Georgie? If you are this nervous you shouldn't be driving today. Shall we ask Mr. Bentley if I can drive instead of you?" she said loudly.

Coming out of the bathroom, a white-faced George replied, "Of course not. I am fine, I must have eaten something bad last night, that's all."

Silvia always called him Georgie when she was annoyed with him. She knew he hated it and that it reminded him of his long-dead brothers.

Once all the regular drivers had finished their qualifying laps, George was allowed out for his run in the Bentley.

A lap of the Le Mans track was 10.726-miles in length; it was narrow and largely tree-lined. Its surface was dusty in fine weather and very slippery when it was wet.

The 3.0 litre Bentley was the biggest and fastest car George had ever driven. After instruction and some advice from team driver Alexander Dumar, he eased into the brown leather driving seat, strapped on his white leather helmet, and pulled down his goggles. He gripped the large steering wheel tightly to make sure Silvia and Hellen, who were watching him, wouldn't notice his hands shaking.

With a swift pull down to the right on the wooden wheel, he turned the great, green car out of the pits. He was off on his Le Mans adventure.

George accelerated the Bentley down the straight narrow road into the outskirts of Le Mans, to the very slow Pontlieue Hairpin bend. Braking hard and slowing down to just 30mph, he turned sharp right before entering the Mulsanne Straight, which George said after his drive,

"went on and on forever".

Increasing speed on the long, long straight, the Bentley, even with George driving, reached 120mph. Rounding the slight right-hand kink towards the end of the straight, George noticed the marker boards for the fast approaching Mulsanne Corner. He lifted his right foot off the throttle and stamped it hard onto the brakes for the tight corner, careful not to touch the sand bank on the outside. He got safely round driving at only 40mph.

Accelerating out of the corner into a funnel of trees, which seemed to suck him along, he raced flat out for another mile down to the right and left turns at Indianapolis Corner. Following a quick blast of acceleration, he once again pressed hard on the brakes to slow down for the ninety-degree right-hand at Arnage Corner. Then full throttle to the very fast and scary curves at White House.

He recalled Alexander Dumar boasting that it takes real guts to go through these blind bends without lifting your right foot off the throttle. Even on that first lap, George knew he would never be able to do that.

From White House he drove flat out once more for over a mile, until he flashed past the pits to start another high-speed lap.

George was enjoying the experience, although his best lap was over two minutes slower than the Bentley team drivers.

That night, when all alone in his bed, George became depressed thinking about his laps of the Le Mans circuit. For the first time in his life, he was aware that he would never be a top-class racing driver. He had scared himself on every lap through the fast curves, especially at White House, and after his five laps he was completely exhausted.

Silvia had said nothing to him after his run, but Hellen, who had been watching from the pits, said,

"Well done, George, you look really dashing behind the wheel." Then she planted a soft, wet kiss full on his lips. Now, licking his lips, George thought that was the best moment of the whole day.

He thought of Hellen as he drifted off to sleep.

It was very hot, almost tropical, for the Le Mans 24 hours, but after much drama and hard racing, Bentley won the race. Of course, there were wild celebrations that evening. Silvia, having drunk too much, ended up in the bed of Alexander Dumar, one of the winning drivers. Seeing his wife go off with Alexander, an angry and champagne-fueled

George took one of the pretty, young French girls who had been invited to the party back to his hotel room for the night. But it was not a success.

Despite her helping hands, George was unable to perform. His mind was elsewhere.

Hellen didn't stay for the party, as she had to rush back to Paris to carry out her dancing duties.

"I will come to England soon, George," she said, before she left. "Be sure to look me up." She then blew him a kiss before jumping into her borrowed Talbot Darracq car.

From the moment of that soft kiss, Hellen was the only woman George could think about. He knew he had to have her.

This Le Mans weekend was the start of the open marriage of George and Silvia. It was an accepted part of the society they mixed in that affairs were going to happen. The need for fun, music and excitement during the early twenties was, in part, a reaction to the harshness and deprivation of the war years. Silvia was in great demand by all the smart young men of the London set.

In 1925, Silvia became pregnant again and, in February 1926, just nine months after their Le Mans trip, she gave birth to a healthy, dark-haired baby girl whom they named Victoria. The fact that she grew up to look nothing like George was never mentioned in the Marshall family, although that didn't stop the cheaper daily papers speculating on who the most likely father was.

The young Marshalls were a newsworthy couple, but Silvia didn't care what the reporters wrote, and George pretended not to notice.

15

It was fortunate for Frank that Howard Jones had travelled
to the Isle of Man in 1927. He'd wanted to be there to
witness Frank's moment of glory. Doctor Jones was able to
organise a private room and the best possible treatment for
his injured friend. The hospital had been busy this year.
Two riders had been killed and seven were in hospital,
including Frank, with broken bones.

After the race, with Frank safely in hospital, Howard Jones
went with Peter to collect the crashed Norton from the
accident site.

It was around 8pm before they found the bike. High on the
bleak mountain road a gusty wind was driving fine salty rain
from the sea and it was getting dark. When he saw the
Norton, Peter slumped down on the granite bolder
supporting the stricken bike.

"The bastards, they have stolen the engine. That was
the best engine Frank had ever built," he said, before
starting to cry.

Doctor Jones put his arm around Peter's shoulder.

"Don't worry, Pete, you know Frank will be back.
He's a real fighter."

Privately, having seen the damage to Frank's knee, Howard
was aware that the patella bone had been fractured in three
places. Frank would be lucky to walk again. For certain he
would never have enough strength in his leg to race a
motorbike.

Howard had sent a telegram to Joan telling her about the
accident, and that Frank's injuries were serious but not life
threatening. The following morning, after ensuring Frank
was comfortable, the two despondent men travelled home

in the van with the sad remains of the Norton dumped in the back. It was a somber, slow journey.

Howard Jones had never married. Having grown up in Lancashire, he had won a scholarship to Cambridge University to study medicine. When he qualified he wanted to stay in East Anglia. He had no plans to return to his northern industrial roots. After his graduation he spent some time looking around for work.

In September 1905, old Doctor McKenzie, who had run the practice covering the villages of Farewell, Burlham and two other small villages a few miles outside Cambridge for over thirty years, died after suffering a heart attack.
The post for a new doctor was advertised in the Cambridge Evening News and the newly-qualified Doctor Jones applied, more in hope than expectation. Much to his surprise, after a short interview, he was accepted for the job. The doctor's house he was allocated, called The Cedars, was located in Farewell.
The Cedars was a large, four-bedroom brick property, which had been built in the early part of the nineteenth century. One of the downstairs rooms had been converted into a surgery, another into a waiting room. Doctor Jones had a housekeeper and a cook, who were inherited from Doctor McKenzie. Both middle-aged women were set in their ways and between them they ran the house.
Howard Jones came from a family where his mother had dominated his every move, so the arrangement felt quite natural to him.

With his slight fear of women, Howard was not looking forward to meeting Joan and Margaret when he returned from the Isle of Man.

The first time he had contact with the Cartland family had been soon after he arrived when Joan visited the surgery one day in 1906. She held the hand of a skinny little boy, who had his left arm in a sling.

When Howard first saw Joan, his heart had given a little jump. She looked like a young version of his mother.

"Hello, young man, you look a bit worse for wear," he said to the boy, who looked down at the floor and said nothing.

"His name is Frank," explained Joan. "He is my young brother and he has fallen over and hurt his arm."

"Let's have a look at you then, Frank," said Doctor Jones. "Please take your shirt off."

Joan helped Frank out of the sling and his shirt.

"My...you do seem to have been in the wars, Frank," Howard Jones said. He tried not to show his surprise at the number of bruises covering Frank's body.

"Let's have a look at this arm."

Frank hadn't uttered a word as the doctor examined it.

"You haven't broken your arm lad, so that's good news. I'll give you a new sling. Keep it there for a week, then come back to see me. Now wait outside while I have a chat with your sister."

Frank went and sat on a chair in the waiting room. On the table he saw a magazine with the word Autocar in large letters written on the cover, which also had a picture of a strange, horseless carriage racing along a dusty road.

Inside the surgery, Doctor Jones said,

"I'm rather concerned about all those bruises on your brother's body, Miss ... sorry, could you tell me your name?"

"I'm Joan Cartland, Doctor. Frank is always getting into scrapes. You know what young boys are like."

"Are you sure that's where he has got all the marks?"

"Yes, I'm sure," said Joan sharply. She was too afraid of her father to tell Howard Jones the truth.

Not wishing to alarm her, Howard Jones said, as he opened the surgery door for Joan,

"Well, please bring him back next week, I would like to see how his arm is healing."

They were surprised to see Frank still engrossed in Autocar magazine.

"You can take that with you if you like, Frank," said Howard Jones.

"Really!" said Frank excitedly "Tha...thank you, Doctor Jones."

Joan gave Howard Jones a big smile as she followed her little brother out of The Cedars.

From that first meeting, Howard Jones had been in love with Joan, but he had always been too shy to ask her out. Now more than ten years had passed since she had lost her only love, Norman Crowe. Those years had not been kind to her, but to Howard she was still the handsome, young woman he had first fallen in love with. Following Frank's accident, though, for once, he wasn't looking forward to seeing Joan.

His first call was at Ivy Cottage to see Margaret; with relief he found that Joan was there with her. It meant he wouldn't have to face two angry women separately and could answer all their questions at once.

"Tell us the truth. Is he going to live?" Margaret said, opening the door before Howard had time to knock.

"Yes, he is, but I think it will be a long, slow recovery. They will be keeping him in the Isle of Man hospital for at least two more weeks."

"Good, let's hope it teaches the stupid, selfish fool a lesson," said Margaret, before bursting into tears.
Joan, with her arms around Margaret, said,

"Thank you, Doctor Jones, I know you have always done your best for Frank"

"Ca … call me Howard," Doctor Jones said, feeling foolish. "I will come and let you know when I have some more news."
He quickly left the two women alone in each other's arms.

The pain and misery that Frank felt for the two days after the accident were intense. The recognition that one small mistake had cost him so dearly was hard to bear. He'd been so very close to victory and that one thought continued to dominate his mind.
The only release he could get from the severe pain in his knee came from the regular doses of morphine he was given. The sensation of euphoria as the needle injected the magic liquid into his veins was certainly addictive. He could feel the pain easing and just drifting away.
I'm rushing down the track, throttle twisted wide open. My eyes are unblinking and focused on the narrow strip of road ahead … trees, walls and the blur of people flash by. The Norton engine is singing to me once again.
We are going to win
We are going to win
We are going to win

I roar across the finishing line as the chequered flag comes down. The crowd is cheering and the champagne flows as I lift the TT winner's Silver Trophy…

A sharp pain shot through Frank's knee, bringing him back to reality.

"Nurse, nurse, come here quick. I need more morphine, now", became his regular desperate appeal.

Frank had to spend three weeks in the Isle of Man hospital. His shattered kneecap required two long operations to wire the bones back together. He also had to have his leg pinned and set before he was transported back to Addenbrooks Hospital in Cambridge.

With a lift from Doctor Jones in his new Morris Minor saloon car, Joan brought Mary and her little sister Emily to see their father in Addenbrooks.

"Is your motorbike hurt as well". The first thing Mary said to her father.

With watery eyes Franks replied

"It is my dear girl…even more than me I'm afraid".

Margaret had refused to visit the hospital while Frank made his long, slow recovery.

On his return home a few weeks later, Frank was welcomed enthusiastically by Mary, and especially by Spike. Even though he was now seventeen years old, Spike excitedly performed his party trick - jumping high in the air and howling.

Margaret's reception was, however much as he expected.

"You bloody fool," she said when the girls were out of earshot. "I hope this has taught you a lesson."

Dejectedly Frank shuffled off into his quiet, dark workshop. Standing there with the help of his walking stick, he looked over to the corner of the room. The remains of his beautiful Norton were leaning against a bench.

It was the first time he had seen the bike since the moment he had passed out up on Isle of Man mountain. His last thoughts had been of relief that the bike had stopped and didn't look too bad. Now he saw that the impact with the granite boulder had turned the Norton's chassis banana-shaped. Pete had already informed him that the engine had been stolen.

It's only good for scrap metal now, he thought. *Even I can't repair that.*

With his knee hurting like hell, it was at that moment when Frank knew he would never race a motorbike again. The Isle of Man TT win would remain just a dream.

Depressed, he turned and went back into the cottage to give Margaret the news.

"Margaret. I'm sure you will be pleased to know that I've ridden in my last motorcycle race." he said with obvious sadness.

"Oh, Frank, you know I'm pleased. I've been waiting five years for you to say that. Maybe I can stop worrying about you every day now and we can have a normal family life."

Frank's announcement delighted Margaret. She would have him home for good, now that his wild days were over forever.

While stuck in hospital, Frank had been lucky his young mechanic Pete Betts could run the garage for him. Pete shared Frank's love for mechanical things.

Pete was the youngest son of farmer Albert Betts but preferred the garage to the farm. Pete kept the garage open and sold petrol while Frank was recovering. This at least brought some money in for the Cartland family, although Frank did have the comfort of knowing that Margaret's father would never see his family starve. They would always have bread to eat.

He knew now he would have to get back to hard work and start building plenty of new engines.

For the following months, Frank concentrated on building up the garage business and keeping his customers happy. All thoughts of racing were banished to the back of his mind as his injuries slowly healed.

Watching Margaret washing up after dinner one evening, Frank thought she must have been having too much of her father's lovely fresh bread. He was sure that she was plumper than when he had returned home a few weeks earlier.

In bed that night Margaret had some news for him.

"I am expecting another baby," she said. "It's due in about six months. I've already told mother and father and they are delighted."

"So am I …" said Frank, without much conviction. He loved his two girls but realised that another new baby would cause even more stress and sleepless nights for Margaret.

While Margaret lay lightly snoring Frank, unable to sleep, slipped out of bed and hobbled out to his workshop. As he sat at the workbench where he built his engines, Frank reflected that this was the only place he felt really in control of his life. He could lose himself for hours; polishing and balancing the jewel-like pistons and connecting rods, honing the cylinder bores until they were silky-smooth, and carefully rebuilding his precious engines.

These were his babies.

16

One lunchtime, Frank hobbled down to the Railway Arms, with Joe taking his arm on one side and Spike limping along on the other. The permanent legacy of the Isle of Man accident was that for the rest of his life Frank would walk as if he had a large stone stuck inside his shoe.

This trio made a sad sight as they painfully hobbled and limped their way down to the pub.

Joan had been to the cemetery to put some flowers on their mother's grave. Had she lived, she would have been sixty years old on that very day. Walking back to the forge, Joan noticed her boys from the top of the lane. She stood and watched them with sadness as they went slowly down towards the Railway Arms.

What has life done to us all? Joan thought. *Ten years ago those three would have been laughing, joking and running to the pub. Now those carefree days are long gone.*

She turned and walked back to the empty and dark forge cottage.

Almost everyone in Burlham loved Spike. From his puppy days as the bookie's runner's assistant, travelling with Frank in the wire basket of their old green bike, he had made friends with all who met him. His bark really was worse than his bite, although the bullyboys of Farewell would always have a different opinion. They still bore the scars of Spike's anger.

Even the village butcher, Alan Coles, who was forever chasing Spike away from his back door, had a soft spot for him. Butcher Coles had been one of Frank's best customers when he was a bookie's runner, Spike always had his eye on the strings of pork sausages hanging behind the shop counter. On a day, while Frank and Alan had been discussing the bets Alan wanted to place, Spike had sneaked out of his basket and stolen some sausages. The string was six sausages long, almost too big for Spike's small mouth, but he managed and set off for home.

"Come back you cheeky little mutt," the butcher shouted as he set off in hot pursuit.

Spike ran as fast as his short legs allowed. They tangled with the bouncing sausages but despite that handicap, Spike was fortunately too fast for the well-fed butcher, as he scampered back to the forge cottage.

There he hid under Frank's old bed and enjoyed his meal. Spike really was in the doghouse for a few days, but the sausages had been worth it.

In the snug bar at The Railway Arms, Spike had his own seat. It was a tired-looking, old, white wicker chair, no one else dared to sit in it if they thought there was a chance Spike might be coming into the pub.

After Joe and Frank had had their two pints of mild, and Spike had enjoyed two ashtrays full of his favorite rich, dark stout, the men sat smoking their Woodbines, with the dog curled up in his chair next to them.

All in a happy silence. Their peace was only disturbed when the landlord, Dan Turner, rang the bell and said,

"Time gentlemen, please".

"Right, you two, it's two o'clock. Time we were making our way home," Frank said. "I've got an engine to build".

Joe and Frank got up, but Spike didn't move.

"Come on, Spike, you lazy old dog," said Joe, giving him a poke. Spike still didn't move.

"Drunk too much beer have you, sozzled old dog? I suppose I'm going to have to carry you home," said Frank, putting his arm under Spike to pick him up.

Instantly Frank understood that his old companion had died in his sleep.

The brothers, both in tears, slowly carried their little friend back home to the forge.

For many years, Spike's bed had been an old motorcycle tyre covered in an old grey blanket next to the range in the kitchen. They gently laid him in it and left him for the rest of the day. Curled up, he looked as if he were fast asleep.

Joan gave an agitated and distressed Joe some of the pills Doctor Jones had prescribed to help him calm down, and she sat with him as he cried himself to sleep.

When Frank arrived back at Ivy Cottage, he said to Margaret,

"My Spike died today in the pub. I know he has lived to a great age for a dog, but I'm really going to miss him … he was my best friend."

You always loved that bloody little dog more than me, Margaret thought.

Joe decided that Spike should be buried on the Devil's Dyke, overlooking the racecourse.

"That's the place he always loved best," he said, with tears once again trickling down his cheeks. "He loved spending the day chasing rabbits and just sitting for hours with me."

Everyone agreed that this would be the best place for the burial, and on a sharp but clear autumn day in 1927, they walked with Spike's body for the three miles to the site Joe had chosen.

Frank was amazed that, in addition to the Cartland family, another ten people made the long walk, including Doctor Jones, Constable Clarke and even the butcher Alan Cope, who joked that at least his pork sausages would be safe. More people came to Spike's funeral than they did to fathers' or Johns', Frank reflected.

17

The following two years saw gradual recovery for Frank, both physically and financially.
His engine building skills were still in great demand from his motorcycle-racing customers, and the more races they won, the greater their desire to use a Cartland built engine. With engines and motorbikes scattered all over the place, Frank was fast outgrowing his village garage and workshop.

Without the major expense of his own racing, the family was gradually becoming better off. Margaret had given birth to their third child, a girl whom they named Edith after her aunt. In addition to taking care of the family's needs, Margaret also had the job of chasing all the customers who hadn't paid their bills. This job suited her blunt, black and white approach to life. For the moment, the Cartland household was a happy one.

   "You really are outnumbered in this family, Frank," said a laughing Howard Jones one day. "Now you've got four women to nag you… no, five counting your sister Joan."

   "At least there should be someone to look after me when I'm old and past it,"said Frank.
After his accident on the Isle of Man, and then Spike's death, Frank had lost much enthusiasm for life. He had lost all his old spark and optimism, but now Howard had noticed that some of his friends positivity had returned. He knew that Frank had begun reading motor magazines again and excitedly talking about racing cars and bikes to anyone who would listen.

Although he was still limping, he could also see great improvements in Frank's health.

"I can't imagine you will ever grow old," Howard said to him.

Inwardly, he feared that the accident had done little to quell his friend's speed addiction.

Margaret's steady, happy family life was soon to be ruined once again. Early on an April morning in 1930, the harmony of the village was shattered with the arrival of Frank's great mate Freddie O'Hare. Freddie turned up at the garage with a noisy and very fast new silver Frazer Nash Ulster sports car. He had a proposition for Frank.

"You know how every bugger wants to use your engines, fearless? Well, there's now a workshop next to mine empty at Brooklands. It's a great bloody chance for you to build your engines there, right at the track. How about joining me; also. I need a new riding mechanic; you would be great for the job. I'll give you ten percent of the prize money."

Two seasons previously, Freddie had retired from motorcycle racing and had started car racing. Immediately he became very successful with his special chain-drive Frazer Nash cars, beating many of the more powerful cars and their established Brooklands drivers.

Although his skills as a driver and engineer meant that Freddie was accepted by the posh Brooklands establishment, it was a reluctant acceptance. His approach to life and poor background always made his presence uncomfortable for the privileged majority.

What Freddie had neglected to tell Frank was that he had the workshop space and needed a new riding mechanic because his last one had just been killed while racing in Ireland.

"You don't bloody well expect me to be a passenger again, after what happened at Spa do you?" said Frank

"It's different in a car; completely safe. All you need to do is keep a look out for any faster cars coming past us on the banking. Of course, there wouldn't be many, you know I'm the best bloody driver out there."
Without another thought, Frank replied,

"Okay, Freddie. Let's go and take a look at this workshop."
As he eased himself into the Frazer Nash, Frank shouted across to Pete Betts, who had come out to admire the Nash,

"Look after the place, Pete...oh, and tell Margaret I'll be back this evening."
Freddie engaged first gear floored the throttle and the 1.5 litre engine snarled, rushing them down the long, twisting and dusty roads south to Brooklands. Once again, Frank left home to follow his love for motors and speed.
Margaret, watching from the kitchen window, saw her husband speed away and once again felt helpless. *Selfish, thoughtless fool,* she thought. But inside she had always known that Frank would put his passion for racing and engines before his family whenever he got the chance.

Late that evening, Frank arrived home in a dark-green Morris van with O'Hare Racing of Brooklands painted on each side of it.

"I'm going to move the engine business down to Brooklands, but I will come home at weekends," he announced to Margaret. "Pete can look after the garage up here while I'm away."

"I bet you don't come back at the weekends," said Margaret angrily. "They race at that nasty place all the time.

"If that's the case I will come back in the week," Frank replied defensively. "Anyway, I'll only be away in the racing season."

"That lasts at least six months," Margaret pointed out, "and how the Hell will you have any time to come back if you have all those bloody engines to build?"
Before Frank had time to answer, Margaret added:

"I'm going to bed. You can sleep out here on the sofa."
Frank listened as the church clock struck three. Lying, unable to sleep on the uncomfortable lumpy sofa, he felt guilty but also excited. *I have a wife and three lovely girls, why can't I be happy with just them?* he pondered.
Of course, he knew the answer. Family life had never been quite enough for him - he needed more. With a surge of excitement building inside him, he accepted that the racing drug was forcing him away from home again.
He hadn't dared mention the fact that he had agreed to act as riding mechanic for Freddie at the following weekend's Brooklands Double Twelve race.
The cockerels were crowing next morning as Frank packed a few clothes into his scruffy, old, brown leather bag ready to leave.

"Take me with you, take me with you," cried nine-year-old Mary, clinging to his good leg as he tried to get away. Frank picked her up and gave her a big hug.

"I would take you, dear girl, but you need to stay here, go to school and learn new things. In a few years you will be old enough to come everywhere with me…then you will be my right-hand man."

This was a long running joke between them.

"I'm a girl; you know I'm a girl! I'm going to be your right-hand girl,"

Mary reminded him.

"Promise I'll get the boys to bring you down on some weekends," said Frank as he got into the driving seat of the Morris. Pete Betts had arrived to open the garage; he stood with Mary as Frank drove away.

Margaret, once again, had refused to see Frank off, she stayed in the kitchen. In fact, she hadn't spoken to him since their argument the previous night.

Frank's new workshop and semi-permanent home was set up in one of the many sheds that had sprung up in the lower paddock area inside the Brooklands track. The workshop was long enough for three cars, plus it had a large wooden workbench running all the way down the left hand wall.

There's plenty of room to build my engines, thought Frank. Along the back was a partitioned room large enough for a small single bed. It had an old sink and a foldaway table, with two chairs to eat at. This was the place where Frank would be spending most of his nights in future.

The 1930 Brooklands Double Twelve race had attracted 51 starters. Frank was to act as riding mechanic to Freddie in his Brooklands Riley.

"This is bloody great. Flying Freddie and Fearless Frank back together again," Freddie said to Frank with a wide grin, as they lined up on the grid for the start. Frank wasn't so sure. As he squeezed himself into the bucket-like, hard passenger seat, of the Riley he remembered clearly the last time he had partnered Freddie at Spa.

The spectacular mass start saw the jostling pack of angry cars surge towards the first right-hand bend, taking them onto the wide, steep banking. Freddie made a fast start, mixing with the big boys as the mass of cars roared out onto the banking. On reaching full speed, the 1.5-litre engine of the Riley was no match for their powerful 3 and 4-litre engines. But it was a handicap race, and Freddie had worked out the lap times he wanted to attain.

They soon settled into a consistent pace. The race was going well; after the second hour the black Riley was in 8th place overall. Frank found the job of riding mechanic much more enjoyable than his previous experience as a sidecar passenger.

Because the cars had no mirrors, his main job in the race was to warn Freddie of any faster Bentleys and Alfa Romeos coming up behind them. The roar from their engine and the whoosh from the wind made hand signals the only form of communication. Frank would tap Freddie on the shoulder when a Bentley or Alfa approached travelling 40mph faster than their maximum 100mph.

Then it started to rain. It was just a light shower, so it made little difference to the track surface. Freddie continued to drive flat out. He became the fastest on the track as most drivers became more cautious.

The track dried again and after five hours racing, Frank was becoming worried. His body was beginning to feel the effects of the constant pounding it was getting when the Riley landed each lap after being launched by the two large bumps around the rough, Byfleet Banking.
Christ, he thought. *There are another seven hours today and twelve hours tomorrow. I'm not going to be able to manage this.*
Every muscle in his body hurt and his damaged right knee was sending sharp, needle-like pains up his leg every time the car landed. Freddie seemed oblivious and was happily driving flat out, the only way he knew. When we stop again for fuel in two laps' time I'm going to have to tell him I can't carry on, Frank had just decided.
Then fate took over.

Frank wasn't the only one suffering with the rough track. The Riley was also taking quite a beating. They were halfway around the Byfleet Banking when the weld connecting the left-hand front mudguard support to the body cried 'enough'.
It broke and the flapping mudguard, caught by the 100mph wind, was ripped from the car. It flew back, catching Frank on the side of the head as it went past and knocked him senseless. Freddie brought the car down to the base of the banking and drove slowly back to the pits, looking across with concern at his friend, who was slumped next to him.

Coasting to a stop, he screamed at the mechanics,

"Get him out, I think he's dead."

They lifted Frank carefully out of the car and laid him on the pit counter. A thin trickle of blood flowed down the left side of his face. Distraught, Freddie wandered away, muttering to everyone he bumped into.

"I've killed my best friend. Frank's dead, and it's my fault."

A Red Cross nurse arrived at the pits and removed Frank's split helmet. She could see a six-inch slash along his skull, just above his ear. She was gently bathing it when, with a start, Frank came to.

"What happened … where am I?" he asked, trying to get up.

"Lie still," said the nurse sharply. "You've had a heavy blow to your head."

Noticing the movement from his friend, Freddie rushed back to the pits.

"Bloody hell, Fearless, I thought you were dead," he said. "But it looks like they have stopped the race, as there's been a big accident."

"What race?" replied Frank. He was still unable to understand where he was.

"I think one of the Bentleys has crashed, all of the cars are coming into the pits," Freddie explained.

After the Riley mudguard had hit Frank, it had bounced along the track, up into the path of the Bentley being driven flat out by Alexander Dumar, the Le Mans winning driver and the ex-lover of Silvia Marshall.

Travelling at 120mph, Dumar had swerved to the right to miss the large lump of metal hurtling towards him, high on the banking. The right front wheel of the big car ran off the top lip of the track, which flipped the Bentley over, ejecting the unfortunate driver and his riding mechanic, Wilfred Owens.

After that the great, green Bentley slid, still upside down, to a smoking, metal-screaming stop and became wedged at the top of the Byfleet Banking, with the front half pointing skyward and the tail at rest on the track.

The two unfortunate men were thrown over the top lip of the track and plummeted thirty feet down through the branches of the sturdy fir trees, falling like demented balls on a pinball machine. Both died instantly.

Back in the Paddock, Frank had been carried to the first aid hut. With his head bandaged, he tried to leave, but the doctor said, "Hold on, Mr. Cartland, you have suffered a concussion and need to rest."

"I feel fine, I'm off home," said Frank.

The race was abandoned for the day, to be continued the following day.

Freddie retired his car and Peter Betts, who had attended as assistant mechanic for the team, drove a very groggy Frank home to Cambridgeshire.

"What the hell have you done this time?" was Margaret's reaction when she saw his bandaged head and white face. Mary just burst into tears.

"Just leave me in peace," said Frank. "I've had a small bump on the head and I'm going to bed to rest." As he went into their bedroom, he slammed the door.

Margaret questioned poor Pete mercilessly, but to his credit he didn't give his boss away, saying that although he hadn't seen what had happened, he'd been told that a piece of metal had fallen on Frank's head.

For two days Frank suffered headaches and felt a bit dizzy, but by the end of the week he had recovered sufficiently to be on his way back to his Brooklands shed.

Margaret never did find out the real cause of his head injury.

The reputation of Frank Cartland continued to grow. Once established at Brooklands, he became known as the leading engine tuner of smaller engine cars and motorcycles.

With Frank's engines, Freddie O'Hare was the man to beat, and he won many races at the track. All the other drivers were desperate to get their engines built by Frank. Silvia Marshall was one of those drivers.

Frank was just getting into the Morris van to start a rare trip home when Silvia approached him.

Like every other red-blooded male, Frank's first reaction upon seeing this stunning woman was one of intense desire. Of course, Silvia knew exactly the effect she had on men, and had become an expert at using it to her advantage.

"I would do almost anything to try one of your engines in my car," said Silvia, looking Frank directly in the eye.

"And I would love to give you one," said Frank without thinking,

"I'm sure you would!" Sylvia laughed.

"Sor ... sorry, Mrs Marshall" said Frank, embarrassed. "I didn't mean it like that."

"Call me Silvia" she replied giving him a wide smile.

This was the first time Frank's path had crossed with any member of the Marshall family.

It was a path he would later wish he had never crossed.

18

The later years of the 1920's had not been good for George Marshall. He was completely overshadowed by his wife, both in popularity and in driving skill. George spent most of his time in London nightclubs. His favorite haunt was the Astor Club in Berkley Square, where he lavished money on the beautiful young ladies who also frequented it.

After their visit to Le Mans, he had fallen in with the Bentley boys. They did everything to excess and he was delighted to be invited to join them. George had always been slightly overweight, but now that he was eating and drinking to excess he was piling on the pounds, was generally unfit and his fine, blond hair was growing thin.

For all her faults, Silvia still found time to devote to her children. Their son William, whose birth had consolidated her position in the Marshall family, was her pride and joy. It certainly helped that each child had their own nanny. They spent most of their time at Sefton Manor at the insistence of Lady Victoria. With the nannies and twenty servants to help, Silvia was often free to pursue her joint passions of motor sport and handsome young men.

While at the London clubs, George was delighted to meet Hellen Dupery once again. Since their Le Mans meeting, he had thought of her every time he made love.
Now here she was performing in London and looking as beautiful as ever.

Hellen's appearance in London was no accident. She knew her dancing days were coming to end, and her future would be bleak unless she found herself a wealthy husband.
Or failing that a rich lover. In France she had had a long affair with one of the younger sons of the famous automobile designer and manufacturer, Ettore Bugatti, but with her uncertain background and current profession, the family had put pressure on their boy to end the relationship. Hellen decided to try her luck in London.

It was while performing her famous fan dance at the Astor Club that she noticed George in the audience. When her act had finished she quickly went over to his table.

"How lovely to see you again, George," she purred, sitting down very close to him. George greedily sucked in the scent of jasmine from the sensual Shalimar perfume on Hellen's near-naked body. The shine of her skin resembled the glow of a full moon. Her short, blond hair shone and her deep blue eyes swallowed his soul.
Unusually eloquent, George said breathlessly,

"Oh, Hellen, I have thought about you endlessly since we first meet in France. I have wanted to be with you desperately since that moment."
Hellen, who had been anticipating a reaction like this from George, said,

"Oh, George, I have also thought about you often since our meeting at Le Mans."
George, of course, did not pick up the lack of conviction in her voice. Henry Duller, a member of the Bentley Boys, appeared at the table.

"Why, it's Miss Dupery," he said. "It is lovely to see you in England."

George felt nervous. Henry Duller was still very handsome. He had known Hellen, and of course George's wife, Silvia, for some time.

"I hope you are going to join me for dinner this evening when you finish here?" said Henry, without looking at George.

"Sorry, Henry, Hellen is coming for dinner with me," said George boldly. Hellen gave him one of her special smiles, which seemed to say,

"I'm all yours".

George and Hellen started a passionate affair that night, and for the first time since his wedding night and honeymoon, sex was exciting and fun for George.

George knew that Hellen also had a passion for racing, but what he didn't know was that in France she had persuaded her lover to loan her one of the family's beautiful blue cars.

Hellen had already proved herself a competent racing driver and had won many minor races in France while driving Hispano-Suiza cars loaned by various rich admirers.

Always looking for good advertising opportunities for his cars, Bugatti had sent Hellen to Montlhery, the very fast-banked track on the outskirts of Paris.

The French had designed Montlhery after witnessing the success of Brooklands in England. It was just as fast, and just as dangerous.

The plan of Bugatti was for Hellen to try to break the women's land speed record, and this she bravely agreed to do.

Many thought he really expected her to kill herself in the attempt getting her of his son's life for good.

The date chosen for this attempt was early January, in very difficult cold and icy conditions.

"Votre fou, tu vas te tuer (You are mad, you'll kill yourself) said Hellen's best friend, a fellow review dancer Maria Lemick.

"Ne vous inquiétez pas pour moi, ceci est ma grande chance d'être un automobiliste de course
(Don't worry about me, this is my great chance to be a racing motorist) Hellen had replied.

Outwardly she appeared full of confidence, but inwardly she was terrified.

Waiting for the signal to start, and nervously tapping the wood-rimmed steering wheel, this slight figure was dressed in clean white overalls, a white linen helmet and a red scarf that flapped in the swirling wind. Her appearance contrasted sharply with the lead grey winter sky.

The signal came. Hellen, with the car already in first gear, released the clutch, pressed her right foot hard on the throttle and with rear-wheels spinning her nerves now forgotten as she became at one with the beautiful blue machine, the roar of the engine, the gusts of the wind and the pure delight of the drive.

For lap after lap the Bugatti hurtled round and round the lip of the high, concrete bowl, as the engine screamed with joy and Hellen danced the little car over the vast, wide track.

Far below her, sheltering in the sparse stone pits, were a huddle of twenty assorted Bugatti officials, timekeepers, mechanics, and pressmen. In addition, in heavy overcoat and hat, Ettior Bugatti stood watching.

« Eh bien, je dois admettre que, cette fille a du cran »
(Well, I must admit, this girl has guts) he commented to the pressmen.

Hellen kept her speed and her concentration, the icy fingers of the wind clawing at her cheeks as it rushed past. Her shoulders were aching as she held the blue machine on the high line of the steep banking. Finally, a signal from the pits told her to stop.

On the slow lap back to the pits, Hellen was disappointed that the run was over. She doubted if she would be able to experience this unique intense pleasure - a jumbled mixture of excitement, fear, and happiness - ever again.

Despite her feeling of euphoria, she was convinced she had not been fast enough to break the record. But the looks on the faces of her lover Jean Bugatti, the mechanics and the press as she stopped and put the Bugatti engine to sleep, quickly dispelled her fears.

Hellen was now the fastest woman in the world. She had reached more than 197mph. For a moment, Hellen was still annoyed with herself, 200mph *would have sounded much better,* she thought.

The Montlhery success had confirmed Hellen's growing reputation in France as being a star automobile driver as well as a celebrated dancer.

Upon moving to London, she had managed to bring a Bugatti Type 35 with her. The car had been given to her by Ettore Bugatti as a final bribe, hoping to drive her away from the Bugatti family for good.

When she arrived in England, Hellen had gone straight to Brooklands. Frank Cartland's reputation for preparing racecars had already reached French motorsport.

Frank was her target.

When this slim, smiling, stunning blond woman walked into the workshop, all spanners were dropped.

"I would like to speak to Frank Cartland," Hellen announced to the three-open-mouthed mechanics standing in front of her.

"Bonjour Mademoiselle," said Frank, walking towards her. "Je suis Frank Cartland."

Frank's two apprentice mechanics were very impressed. They had never heard their boss speak French before.

"Bonjour, Frank, my name is Hellen Dupery. I have an old car outside and I would like you to run it for me at Brooklands."

Following Hellen out of the workshop Frank was faced with an old trailer hitched to an equally-old Citroen, but on the trailer…a vision. There sat a muddy and well-used 1927 Bugatti Type 35 racing car.

Despite the Bugatti's appearance, Frank's excitement was obvious.

"Oh, Miss Dupery, it would give me great pleasure to work on this beauty," he said. Smiling, he ran his hand gently over the swooping curve of the heaven blue tail.

"Excellent, Frank…please call me Hellen. How much money do you want from me to prepare Bleu Bebe?"

As she spoke, Hellen gave Frank one of her wide, seducing smiles.

"What's Bleu Bebe?" asked Frank.

"It's my name for this Bugatti, she's my baby," said Hellen.

"Let's not worry about the cost now er…Hellen, we will get the Bugatti into the workshop. The boys can clean it up and I'll look at the engine."

Hellen had expected the Bugatti to have this effect on Frank. In fact, she was banking on it. She had arrived in England almost penniless.

Having entrusted the Bugatti into the care of Frank Cartland, Hellen went straight up to London, where she had bumped into George Marshall again. With her meeting with Frank and her seduction of George, Hellen's move to England was going even better than she could have hoped.

Before long, Hellen was making a name for herself and Bleu Bebe at Brooklands. In her skillful hands, the pretty, blue Bugatti proved to be very quick and competitive.
The motoring press wasted no time in inventing a strong rivalry between Silvia and Hellen. These two beautiful and fast ladies quickly became headline news. All the newspapers built up the story that George Marshall's wife and his lover were competing for him on and off the racetrack.
In fact, Silvia and Hellen liked each other. They had very similar personalities, and had a good laugh at the situation, much to the discomfort of George.

Both also enjoyed the sexual pleasures of other women and were mutually attracted to each other. They decided to have some fun at George's expense. Hellen had told Silvia that George was planning to take her to the Ritz for dinner, followed by a night of passion.
Hellen let her know their room number and they agreed that Silvia would come into the hotel room using a spare key at exactly 10pm. Hellen would make sure that she and George were naked in bed at that time.

The night arrived, and all went to plan. George and Hellen had feasted on oysters and champagne. They were very merry as they started to make love. Meanwhile, Silvia crept into the room and feigned shock at seeing her husband with her friend.

"Oh, George, how could you do this to me!" she exclaimed

Momentarily perturbed, George looked startled, like a rabbit trapped in headlights. Then Hellen said, laughing,

"Hello Silvia, why don't you join us?"

Without hesitation, Silvia stripped off her clothes and jumped onto the bed with them. Still in shock, George could only watch as the two beautiful women immediately began passionately kissing. They quickly moved onto caressing and kissing each other's breasts and hardening nipples. Then they took up Silvia's favorite sixty-nine position and used their tongues to please each other. They groaned with pleasure as they did so.

With Hellen's beautiful round bottom close to him, it was too much for George, as the two girls moaned with pleasure he took himself in hand.

George really couldn't believe his luck that two of the most beautiful women in England were here with him. It was, he thought, one of the best nights of his life.

Unfortunately, George's life wasn't always going to be this happy.

The girls continually goaded him about his lack of racing success. All their Brooklands racing driver friends had achieved the coveted 120mph record badge. This was awarded to all drivers who could average this speed over three laps of the Brooklands full circuit. The colourful metal, enamelled badge was proudly carried on the front of their road-going Bentleys and Lagondas.

"Oh, Georgie, come and look, the 120mph Brooklands badge is not on the front of your car…has someone stolen it?" Silvia asked.

This became a regular joke between the two women in George's life.

19

Silvia had started racing at Brooklands in 1927, the first year
The Brooklands Automobile Racing Cub (BARC) allowed
women to race with the men, and she was immediately
successful in small handicap races.

For the 1931 season she had brought a new car, on the
recommendation of Freddie O'Hare. The car was a dark-
green Frazer Nash.

After their previous conversation, Silvia went to see Frank
Cartland with a large wad of cash.

Walking through the open door of his workshop, she found
him with his head deep under the bonnet of a customer's
MG.

"Hello again, Frank, are you ready to give me one
now?" she said, waving the cash.

Frank straightened up with a start, and banged his head on
the edge of the MG's bonnet. Rubbing it, he said,

"Ah, Mrs. Marshall, er Silvia. Wh....what can I do for
you?"

"I want you to build me an engine. Whatever it takes,
I want you to give me your best one," she said

After their first encounter, Frank was careful with his reply.
Still rubbing his sore head, he said,

"I always build all my engines with love and care. I
will, of course, do the same for yours."

Silvia moved close to Frank and teasing him replied,
Taking his hand in hers she said

"I can see that you have sensitive and strong fingers,
so I'm sure that you will give me a good one. I'll get one of
the boys to drop the car in tomorrow."

Leaving the money on the seat of the MG, she was laughing as she turned and walked slowly back out of the door. Embarrassed again, Frank muttered,

"I'll do my best, Mrs. Marshall," as he watched his visitor's shapely figure disappear out of his workshop door.

The first race Silvia competed in with the new engine was a 4-lap handicap, which she won with ease.

That victory insured she was given a very hard time for any future handicap races, but this didn't worry her. Silvia had already decided that she and her good friend Hellen Dupery would enter the Frazer Nash for the Brooklands Double Twelve. This was the hardest and most prestigious race of the year.

It was a thousand-mile race run over two days, with five hundred miles to be covered each day. Most people, including her husband George, thought she was mad.

"No woman could concentrate long enough to win that race," George complained to his mother.

"Well, you should be a man and stop her then," said Victoria Marshall dismissively. Victoria had given up trying to understand her daughter-in-law many years ago. Now she had as little to do with her as possible.

Experience had taught her that she couldn't manipulate Silvia the way she could control her son.

She also knew that George had no chance of stopping Silvia doing anything if she had made up her mind to do it.

Frank, and Freddie O'Hare had thought that it was a great idea for the girls to share the driving of the car in the Double Twelve race.

"Just think of the publicity when they win the Brooklands Double Twelve?" an ever-optimistic Freddie said to Frank.

"With my car preparation and your engine, the girls can't bloody lose."

The race was held on 24th and 25th May. The large prize fund, attracted an entry of 37 cars. These included 6-litre Bentleys, 3-litre Talbots, 2-litre Lagondas, 1.5-litre Alfa Romeos, Lea Francis, Aston Martins and Frazer Nash, down to the 1,000cc cars, which included the Riley of Silvia Marshall and Hellen Dupery.

The race started without major incident and towards the end of the first day, as 500 miles approached, the Riley was going strongly both girls driving steadily at their agreed pace.

Then disaster struck the race. Two of the Talbot cars were racing close together when they collided. This was just after they had overtaken Hellen driving the Riley.

One Talbot reared into the air and Hellen swerved and missed the big green car by inches. The Riley went into a slide but with great skill Hellen corrected the skid, regained control, and continued out onto the banking for another lap. Behind her the Talbot driver lost complete control of the green car which careered into the public enclosure opposite the pits. The hapless driver, Colin Marsh, was thrown out and killed instantly. To the crowd's horror he was impaled on the spiked railing bordering the track. Meanwhile, the driverless Talbot ran into the crowd and three spectators were killed.

Sensational headlines that night in the London papers demanded that the race be stopped. But it went on the next day as planned.

"You must retire now," said a red-faced George Marshall as he had dinner that evening with Silvia and Hellen. "I forbid you to carry on with this madness. One of you could get killed."

The girls were unusually subdued. But, though shaken by the incident and tired after 500 miles of racing, they were determined to continue.

"It's so sweet of you, Georgie, but we are big girls now, we can take care of ourselves," said Silvia.

"We have had our close shave in this race, so tomorrow will be fine," added Hellen.

They had every intention of being on the starting grid the following morning.

The day dawned bright and clear, all the dramas of the previous day soon forgotten by the drivers. The little Riley buzzed quickly around the concrete bowl, never missing a beat.

Both girls were driving fast but taking no risks, while most of the other, bigger cars, struck trouble with engines misfiring, punctures, and a few accidents.

Fortunately, none of these were serious and there were no more injuries.

Both ladies were dirty and tired when the chequered flag waved to single the end of the race, but they were ecstatic, just finishing this hard and punishing race a real achievement.

When the results were announced, the girls discovered they had finished 4th overall behind three Talbots.

With everyone congratulating them on their success, a further announcement was made that although Silvia Marshall and Hellen Dupery had finished 4th overall on distance in their Riley, they had been placed 1st on handicap, having averaged 84.41mph.

Before the event the handicap committee had spent hours calculating and setting the handicap for each car.

Silvia and Hellen deserved their win.

Now clean and looking glamorous they accepted the magnificent Double Twelve Trophy at the prize-giving dinner that evening.

Champagne flowed all night in the Brooklands clubhouse, although by 10pm George had gone home to bed ... alone.

20

By 1933, George had become fed up with being the butt of his famous wife and his equally-famous lover's jokes. The final straw had been as he listened to his old school mate, Allister McApline, boasting in the Brooklands clubhouse after he got his 120mph badge.

"Remember all those years ago, Georgie, back at Leamington School? he said. "We talked about racing at Brooklands and I told you I would beat you. Don't suppose you will ever get a 120mph badge.
"

Now George had decided that it was time he had some motor racing glory himself. Knowing he didn't have the skill to win any major races, he commissioned, at great personal expense, the building of a powerful car suitable to help him obtain that coveted 120mph badge.

How hard can it be to keep your foot flat down for a few laps? he thought.

The car was a development from one of the old Le Mans winning Bentleys. George had recently purchased it from the Bentley works. His mechanics had rebuilt the car George had named the Marshall Crusader. The mighty machine was painted deep red, with the Marshall coat of arms on both sides of the bonnet. Everyone told George he should have the special 4.5-litre supercharged engine rebuilt by Frank Cartland, so George went to his workshop at Brooklands.

Although he knew Frank had been building his wife's engines and was looking after his lover's Bugatti, George had deliberately avoided talking to Frank in the past.

I certainly have nothing in common with him, he thought to himself.

In fact, Brooklands was not the first occasion Frank and George had seen each other, although neither of them remembered the first time.

Their first meeting had come at Newmarket Racecourse, when Frank was ten and George was just eight.

Joe had taken Frank to the Newmarket races, as he often did in those days. They had walked the three miles along the Devil's Dyke to the racecourse. Between races they would play, running up and down the steep banks of the dyke and tumbling into the ditch.

When the horses came out of the paddock, they would run to the start and watch the magnificent thoroughbreds and their colourful jockeys as they lined up behind the starting tapes. Frank loved the drama of the start, with each jockey straining and pushing their great mounts into the best positions. Then the tapes would go up with a sharp, whip-like snapping sound.

Sometimes they would run to the rail on the outside of the track and crane their necks to glimpse the finish of the race as the horses charged passed. Resting from their play, Frank and Joe were leaning on the rail and looked across the track to the enclosures where the rich, well-dressed, paying spectators were.

Peering back at them, and standing all by himself, was a sad little blond boy dressed in a tweed suit with tie and waistcoat.

"Look at that poor little sod, he must be boiling dressed like that," said Joe.

"I'm glad I've only got on vest and shorts," Frank said.

George was hot and he was very bored; he hated horse racing. He had wished he could be like that scruffy little boy on the other side of the racecourse, running about free and happy.

Frank was just finishing refitting a fresh engine into Hellen Dupery's Bugatti when George Marshall marched into the workshop, his three mechanics close behind.

"Cartland, I want you to stop whatever you are doing and start work on rebuilding my new engine."

Frank slowly turned to look directly at George, and said,

"Good afternoon to you, too, Mr. Marshall."

Then he put his head back under the bonnet of the Bugatti. Like most of the racing community, Frank deliberately didn't address George as "the Honorable".

"My men here can have the engine with you tomorrow," George continued. "I will expect it back rebuilt to the highest standard in two weeks."

Frank stood up and looked straight at George.

"If I agree to rebuild your engine, Mr. Marshall, you must agree to run it as I say," he said. "And you will get it back when I think it's ready, not before."

George was taken aback. He wasn't used to being spoken to like that. Usually people just did what he told them to do.

"Er, very well, we have a deal," said George. Then he turned and walked out of the workshop, his men following close behind.

Six weeks before the meeting in which George planned to reach the 120mph lap, Silvia and Hellen had had a thrilling race. Silvia beat Hellen for the first time, winning by just one car's length. The engine she used had been specially rebuilt that week by Frank Cartland.

That evening after a celebratory bottle of champagne, a happy Silvia decided to thank Frank for his skills.
Frank had, of course, been given a small share of the prize money after their famous Double Twelve victory the previous year.
He deserves a special prize now, Sylvia thought giggling to herself.
Frank was sitting alone in his workshop resting after a hectic day's work. Quietly smoking a Woodbine, he was very surprised when Silvia tottered in.

"I've got a present for you, Frankie," she said, weaving her way, a little unsteadily, between the still hot metal of her winning Riley and Hellen's beautiful Bugatti.

"It's to say thank you for building me such wonderful engines."
Frank noticed that she was wearing black high-heeled shoes and a large, golden, fox fur coat. *It's a bit hot to be wearing a coat like that,* he thought.
Silvia stopped in front of Hellen's Bugatti, only six-feet from Frank. Then she turned to face him and opened the coat to reveal her stunning and gleaming naked body.

"Come and get your present, Frankie," she said.
Frank couldn't take his eyes off her.
Since his night with Susan in the Isle of Man, he hadn't been unfaithful to Margaret. Surrounded by girls and women at home gave him a respect for them which meant

that even when sex was offered to him on a plate, he was able to resist it. But this was different. There was no emotion involved and Frank simply didn't have time for thought or guilt. This was pure lust.

Throwing away his half-smoked Woodbine, he walked right up to Silvia and cupped her pendulous breasts in his oily hands. He breathed in the sensual fragrance of her Chanel perfume as she pushed him away slightly and arched her back over the lovely curved, warm tail of Hellen's blue Bugatti. She then slid both hands into a gap in Frank's overalls and, pulling hard, ripped them apart. The steel buttons burst over the workshop floor, one pinging off the blue paintwork of the Bugatti.

"I hope that didn't scratch the paintwork, my lady," said Frank with a smile.

In one swift movement Silvia dragged aside his pants, and his already-erect penis sprung out from the gaping overalls.

"My, Frankie, you are not very tall, but you sure are a big boy."

Frank only had one thought as Silvia grabbed his throbbing member and guided it straight into her. For Frank, with that exquisite sensation came the vision of one of his beloved lightened pistons gliding up and down in the beautifully-honed bores of his best engine. Faster and faster went the piston, the revs increasing until the mixture exploded right at the top of the stroke.

Silvia let out a high scream and for that moment nothing but pure pleasure existed for either of them. Coming back to reality, Frank felt a strange dampness spreading down his legs. He looked down and noticed a large wet patch growing on his overalls. He pulled away quickly and stood with a rapidly-lowering penis. It was shrinking like a large slug hit by a sprinkling of salt. Frank had a look of bewilderment on his face. Seeing Frank's shocked expression, Silvia said, with a deep laugh,

"What's the matter, Frankie, have you never had a golden shower before? You should be very pleased with yourself. That doesn't happen to me very often."
Unable to speak, Frank watched as Silvia unwrapped herself from the curvaceous, blue tail of the Bugatti.
She gave him a quick peck on the cheek and pulled her fur coat back around her shoulders. Without a backward glance, she walked away and out of the workshop.
Frank knew this hadn't been a dream … his legs were soaking wet.

That night Frank drove home to his Cambridgeshire village. By the time he arrived at Ivy Cottage it was after midnight. Margaret was already in their bed, asleep.
Getting into bed beside her Frank, remembering the surprising event he had recently experienced, felt himself getting hard. He turned towards Margaret and pressed against her warm, soft body. Pulling up her nightdress, he pushed himself between her legs. It had been some months since they had last made love.
"You must have had a good day," Margaret murmured sleepily, welcoming the unexpected attention. Frank soon climaxed deep inside his wife. All the while he was thinking about Silvia and the unexpected present he had received. They both turned over and Margaret went straight back to sleep.
Frank lay with his eyes open in the inky darkness of their bedroom. With no moonlight, it was the type of darkness in which your mind builds its own shapes. With Silvia's visit

on his mind, Frank's shapes were the sensuous curves of her spooning with the swooping curves of the blue Bugatti. Did that really happen to me? he thought. But he knew it had. Although this time it was not wood smoke he could smell on his skin, it was the flowery fragrance of Silvia's perfume.

He also knew he could never tell anyone about the day's experiences. He could imagine Freddie's reaction if he told him.

"Bloody hell fearless you must have been having one of your weird dreams again. A wet one this time. Silva Marshall wouldn't touch you with a barge-pole! "

No…he was sure no one would ever believe him.

21

Six weeks later, they were all back at Brooklands to witness George's attempt to win his 120mph badge. George had persuaded his parents, Lord and Lady Marshall, to come along to support him. They had, with reluctance, agreed. Silvia brought their 10-year-old son, William, to experience his first motor race.

William had recently been taken by his grandmother for his initiation at the tomb of his ancient ancestor.

"I can understand why the ceremony seems so important to you, grandmother," he'd said to Victoria as she led him out of the Templar Chapel after his stone kiss and bloodletting.

"I have great respect for the family history, but to me just being a Marshall will be enough to make sure I carry on the family name."

Before the trip, his mother had told him how his father had been frightened when he had been taken for his initiation.

"The whole tradition is out of date, it's stupid," Silvia had said to him.

William, even at ten years old, had his own ideas. He had never been close to his father, who didn't seem to be able to talk to him as a father should. Most of the time I feel more grown up than he appears to be, he thought.

He was, however, very excited about the trip to Brooklands, and he was looking forward to being able to boast to his school chums about his father's racing success.

Around 10am on the morning of the record attempt, George entered Frank's workshop with his family and hangers-on. He was keen to show off his new racing car. An excited William ran up to the gleaming, red machine and went to jump into the seat.

"Don't touch it!" shouted his father sharply, halting William in his tracks. William stood, feeling embarrassed and disappointed, next to the large, brown leather seat, while everyone stared at him.

Already tucked into the corner of the driving seat, sat Bertie, his father's scruffy, old brown bear. William felt a pang of jealously. *He thinks more of that scruffy old bear than he does of me,* he thought.

Breaking the awkward moment, Frank appeared from the back of his workshop.

"Ah, everyone, this is my man, Cartland," George explained to his entourage.

"He has rebuilt the wonderful new engine in the Marshall Crusader to my specification." Frank ignored him, and gave William a knowing smile as he walked past to get a spare set of spark plugs from his workbench. George continued showing off his car to the party.

Frank had been really looking forward to his next encounter with Silvia. He'd had glimpse of her as he walked across the workshop. She looked sensational in a low-cut, cherry-red dress, which was almost the same shade of red as the racing car.

He'd been instantly aroused. Frank wearing brand-new, sparkling-white overalls, had washed and slicked back his hair. He'd even scraped most of the dirt out from under his fingernails. When she saw him, Silvia, out of the rest of the Marshall family's earshot, said,

"My God, Frank, what have you done to yourself. I preferred you when you were … dirty."
With the viewing finished, the Marshall group filed out of Frank's workshop behind George. Silvia gave Frank a wink as they went off to the clubhouse bar for drinks.

"Make my tea, Cartland, my good man," said a voice from the back of the workshop. Freddie O'Hare had been standing out of sight for the whole time the Marshalls were present.

"Fuck off, Freddie," replied Frank sharply. He was disappointed at Silvia's reaction to seeing him all smartened up.

"Don't worry about that stupid bugger, George Marshall," said Freddie, "it doesn't look like his family like him any more than the rest of us. Tell you what, I'll make the tea."
That did make Frank smile. Freddie's special tea always had a large slug of cheap brandy in it.
They stood drinking their beverage next to the beautiful, streamlined Marshall Crusader.

"I think even with my bad leg I could drive this beauty round Brooklands at 120mph," Frank remarked. "George Marshall should have no trouble."

"Don't be so sure, I wouldn't trust that stupid bugger to drive 100 yards without hitting something," was Freddie's reply.

At noon, George went out for his practice run. He did four fast laps but was still almost 5mph slower than his target of

120mph. George drove the car back into the paddock fast, sliding the rear wheels and spraying the startled spectators with gravel. He stopped next to Frank and his mechanics. Red-faced, he jumped out of the car before raging at Frank.

"Cartland, your bloody engine is no good, it needs more revs," he screamed.

"The engine is fine…it's more likely to be your crap driving," muttered Frank in reply. George pretended not to hear this. He had his three mechanics nearby. They were already checking the hot car.

"Strip down the back axle and get that axle ratio changed so that I can rev this bloody useless engine some more," George shouted at them

"Hang on lads, the safety limit for this engine is only built for 4000 revs maximum," said a startled Frank.

"You can't let them change the axle ratio. If you do, the engine will likely blow up." he added to George. The scar on Frank's forehead had turned bright pink.

"It's my bloody car, I'll do what I like with it," George shot back. "And they work for me, so they will do whatever I tell them to do."

"We had a deal that you would run that engine as I say," said Frank, then added, "but it's your bloody funeral." He turned away and quickly limped back to his shed in disgust.

Frank was having a cup of tea and a smoke when Freddie came rushing in.

"I've just seen those Marshall lads stripping the back axle on the Crusader. Has something broken?" he asked.

"No that idiot George Marshall has told them to put a higher ratio in so he can use more revs." Replied Frank

"Fucking fool," was all Freddie said.

22

The record attempt had been heavily advertised by the Brooklands promoters, and a large crowd was present at the meeting. After the last race of the day, George Marshall prepared for his run. Silvia was in the Paddock to make a show for the photographers gathered around the car. To demonstrate her support in front of the press, she gave her husband a final kiss onhis lips. But as George pulled on his white leather helmet and lowered his racing goggles she whispered to him,

"Go on, Georgie, now show me you aren't the coward I think you are."

Angry, George slammed the car into first gear and, with the rear tyres squealing in protest, turned the bright-red, flame-spitting Marshall Crusader out onto the vast home straight. With a clenched jaw and fixed stare he gave Bertie, who was tucked down next to him, a final squeeze before flooring the throttle. George was determined to average the 120mph lap needed to get his badge. He would never have admitted it to anyone, but he felt scared and very lonely. His heart was thumping so hard it felt like it would burst out of this chest.

George knew that on the practice run earlier he had panicked and lifted his foot off the throttle as the car drifted towards the top of the high, Byfleet Banking. He also knew that this was the real reason he hadn't been able to reach top speed - there wasn't any fault in the engine. This time, he thought, I will not lift my foot whatever happens.
The first lap went well as he built up speed. With the extra revs allowed by the change of axle ratio, the engine responded well. By the end of the second lap the announcer excitedly shouted the speed.

"119mph, just 1mph to go for George Marshall" George, to his own amazement, had a growing confidence that he was going to succeed. The Marshall Crusader just a red flash as it roared past the paddock crowds. The sound of the high whine coming from the super-charged engine was evidence to all that George still had the throttle wide open
As the car went out on its final third lap, Frank had his binoculars trained on the car.

"Fuck," he said under his breath. He had noticed a telltale light trail of smoke coming from the fish-tale exhaust pipe. He instinctively knew exactly what was happening inside his precious engine. Frank could visualize the pistons pumping up and down inside the bores of the engine. They were now moving faster than they had ever been designed to do. He knew from the smoke that some piston rings had broken under the strain, and that oil was escaping past them into the combustion chamber.

"It's only a matter of time," he muttered to no one in particular.

Lighting another Woodbine, he turned and started slowly walking away from the paddock. He was certain that the poor engine would soon destroy itself, unless George lifted his right foot on this lap.

In the cockpit of the car, George was oblivious to the drama taking place inside the screaming engine in front of him. He was pleased with himself. This time he had managed to keep his foot hard on the throttle all the way around the Byfleet Banking. Halfway through the third lap, the great red car drifted dangerously close to the top lip of the Byfleet banking, but still George managed to keep his right foot flat to the floor. The revs were rising well above their safety limit.

He was grinning as the car roared on to the Home Banking, flashed under the Members' Bridge and across the white timing line. His last thoughts were that the lap must have been much better than 120mph. Then, as he came into full view of the packed paddock, the engine unable to take any more abuse gave up the struggle and blew apart.

Until that moment all the drama had been taking place unseen inside the engine. A poor piston, no longer lubricated by the broken rings, had seized in its bore, but the crankshaft was still turning at more than 4500 revs per minute. The crowd heard the ensuing explosion as it smashed the connecting rod through the side of the cylinder block. Boiling water, steam and hot oil were forced out onto the track, into the cockpit and over the rear tyres of the stricken car. To the crowds in the paddock, the car seemed to magically disappear inside a great cloud of black smoke.

The loud explosion that George heard above the sound of the rushing wind was the first he knew of the disaster, but within a split second his body and face were assaulted by a mixture of scolding water and oil. The rear of the car, already on the edge of adhesion, slid upwards as soon as the oil reached the tyres, George intuitively turned up into the skid. The effect of the banking and his steering correction swung the rear of the red car violently back the other way, and the momentum flung George from his seat high into the air. He was still travelling at more than 90mph when he landed head first on the unforgiving, sloping concrete track. His white leather racing helmet offered him no protection. The heavy impact with the concrete split it, and George's head, like a ripe watermelon dropped onto a hard surface.

Little Bertie had been tucked into the seat next to George and was ejected from the car at the same moment as its owner. The bear was sent flying over the top lip of the banking and into the trees where some branches of a large Norway spruce arrested his flight. Bertie hung there suspended by one long arm, as if looking down on the catastrophic scene as it unfolded below. He even gave the impression of waving.
For two years, Bertie remained stuck in that tree, unnoticed. The branches slowly grew around him, holding the poor little bear fast in their grip.
Then the birds arrived. Magpies came to peck out Bertie's shiny glass eyes and the metal stud in his ear, crows and pigeons to steal his straw. The rain, snow and cold eventually rotted his brown furry body.
Then Bertie just disappeared.

The driverless, smoking, stricken car continued backwards down the steep-banked track, gathering speed as it reached the bowl at the bottom of the slope. Horrified, the crowd suddenly realised that this uncontrolled red monster was heading straight for them and, on mass, turned and scattered in all directions with screams and panic.

In the paddock crowd that day, attending their first car race meeting, were Mr. and Mrs. Smyth. They were sitting in Albert Smyth's pride and joy, their new 1933 Austin 7 Saloon motorcar.

In fact, their real surname was Smith. Albert's wife Madge had persuaded him to   change their name when they married.

"It makes us sound more important," she had said to Albert.

The Austin 7 was the first car that Albert had owned. He had been saving for it over the last two years, putting a little money away each week until he had the £118 needed to buy the car. When he got to the showroom the salesman persuaded him to spend an extra £10 to get the deluxe saloon with real-leather seats. Albert proudly drove the little Austin home with great care. His wife didn't share his love for the vehicle, and she was very angry that he had spent the extra £10.

"You are a stupid man, Albert Smyth. You knew I wanted that new three-piece suit in Harrison's furniture shop window. Now we can't afford it."

Albert kept quiet and went out to polish his new car.

The Smyths' had been invited to Brooklands by the manager of the large south London showroom where Albert had bought his new Austin 7.

Albert had been really looking forward to the trip, as he had dreamt of going to Brooklands for many years. In the week leading up to the event his fellow clerks in the bank, where he worked, joked that they had never seen him so excited about anything.

Disappointingly the day had already been spoilt for him. His wife had hated Brooklands from the moment she arrived. They had left home early for the trip and Albert had found a good spot at the top of the paddock spectators' parking area.

Madge couldn't understand why anyone would want to come to this vast concrete place. It was full of loud, harsh engine noise that hurt her ears, and the pungent smell of burnt oil, which stung her nose. But worst of all were the awful snobbish crowds, with their posh big cars and superior attitudes.

Madge had bought a new hat for the special day, but the wind blew it off the moment she got out of the car. All day the wind remained too strong for her to wear it. She put on her best scarf instead but looking at all the glamorous women in their sharp suits and Hermes scarves, Madge felt completely out of place and very uncomfortable. All she had wanted today was for Albert to take her on a picnic to their quiet spot by the Thames at Windsor. She hadn't wanted to come to this nasty, smelly, unpleasant place.

Now she was in a very bad mood and would not get out of the car. They sat in unhappy silence eating the last of their fish paste sandwiches. Madge was impatient for the gates to open to let them get away. She was desperate to get home to their quiet, little semi-detached house in Richmond.

When she had been making the sandwiches that morning, she had looked forward to the day ahead. Now she had no appetite. Madge wound down the car window to throw her sandwich away.

At least Albert's last thoughts were happy ones. He was in his own little world as he sat in the driver's seat playing with the advance and retard levers on the Austin's steering wheel. He breathed in deeply and the wonderful, rich leather smell coming from the olive-green seats of his beloved little Austin made him smile. *Oh well*, he thought. *At least I've experienced this magical place.*

Upon reaching the bottom of the banking, the Marshall Crusader continued its backward charge until it reached the earth banking that protected the parking areas from the track. The bank acted like a launching pad for the car, which hurtled up it, arcing high over the panic-stricken spectators, and turning over as it flew through the air. It landed, with a large explosion, squarely on top of the shiny Austin 7 containing the hapless Mr. and Mrs. Smyth.

Almost unnoticed, the lifeless body of George Marshall continued its slow slide down from the top of the steep banked track, its progress marked by a snail-like, bright red trail of blood and brains on the stark white concrete. Frank had walked halfway back to his workshop by the time the accident happened. He was intending to pack up and go home, as he anticipated that an angry George Marshall would be towed back in the blown-up car. When the sound of the screams from the crowd reached him, he turned just in time to see the final act of the drama as the Marshall Crusader landed on top of the little Austin 7.

He ran back as fast as his ruined knee would let him…and found himself at a scene of carnage. There was nothing he could do.

Suddenly a jet of hot, rust coloured, water spurted from the broken radiator of the steaming mechanical mess. For a split-second Frank thought. *Looks like it's taking a piss.*

Then he noticed, next to the smoking wreck, a pearl-white arm severed at the elbow. The fingers on the small hand were still clutching a fish paste sandwich.

Others soon arrived and they all desperately tried to pull the two cars apart, but it was far too late to save Mr. and Mrs. Smyth.

The Marshall Crusader was dragged off the little Austin by the breakdown truck. Remarkably most of the damage to the big red car was superficial.

However, extracting the bodies of Albert and Madge from their flattened Austin 7 was a difficult and traumatic operation. Mechanics cut the roof off the car with hacksaws and found that Albert's upper body had been crushed down onto the steering wheel.

The violent impact had forced the steering wheel so far into his chest that it couldn't be removed. The wheel had to be cut from the Austin's bent steering column, and poor Albert had to be taken to the mortuary with the wheel still embedded in his chest.

The body of Madge, less its left arm, had been compressed down into the passenger side foot-well of the Austin. Most of her bones had been crushed by the impact. Curled into a tiny ball, she looked like a bloody little fetus in the womb.

Mercifully there were only three fatalities from this disaster, although two people broke legs and many others had cuts and bruises sustained in the panic as they rushed away to avoid the stricken car.

The Marshall family had been watching the unfolding drama from the advantage of the balcony on the Brooklands clubhouse. Although they were some way from the crash, it seemed certain that the catastrophic accident had killed George. The reaction of each was interesting. Silvia turned away and gave a soft scream. Then, clutching her stomach, she collapsed into a chair, much to her son William's distress and confusion.

The older Marshalls, John, and Victoria, slowly put down their binoculars and remained standing next to each other in silence.

They had experienced the pain of loss before. Now they had just witnessed, first-hand, the death of their last living son.

Victoria's first thought, looking down into the tear streaked face of her grandson William, was: *Thank God George has had a son.*

William had been very excited when they'd arrived that morning, and he'd had his first sight of the Brooklands track. Unfortunately, his father's attitude towards him had left him disappointed.

He had hoped and expected that his father would have at least let him sit in the great red car. But George had practically ignored his son all morning and had embarrassed him in front of all those people.

Now, with the scenes of chaos outside and the reactions of his family, he was old enough to know that the future direction of his life had changed forever.

The rest of the day was a blur to most of those who were close to the disaster.

Frank went back to his workshop, packed his tools into the Morris van, and drove sadly and slowly back to his Cambridgeshire home. When he got back he became suddenly aware that he couldn't remember any details of the trip.

"You are back early," Margaret commented when he walked into the kitchen ashen-faced. "You never usually get back from that place before midnight. What on earth has happened this time?"

"George Marshall crashed his car, he and some other people have been killed," Frank said. "The engine I built blew up because that stupid bastard over-revved it ... I'm sure there is going to be a lot of trouble."

Frank wasn't normally a drinker, but he went into the front room and poured himself a large whiskey. Margaret stomped in after him.

"Well done! For years you have been trying to kill yourself. Now it sounds like you've helped kill someone else. I hope you're satisfied. Bloody engines and racing have finally ruined our lives.

You are no better than your murderous brother!"

Frank had the whiskey bottle in his hand and his instinct to turn and slam it into the side of his wife's face was very strong. A split second before that action, he turned and, not looking at her, went straight to his garage workshop and locked the doors.

Here in his sanctuary all was quiet and still. Amid the engines, the smells of burnt oils and the faint aroma of exhaust fumes, which he loved, he could relax. He knew his wife would regret that last remark and he didn't hate her for it.

He had grown to expect her to lash out at him when things went wrong.

Bleu Bebe, the heaven-blue Bugatti, was sitting at the back of the workshop, where Frank had left her when he brought the car up from Brooklands two days earlier. Two days, seems a lifetime ago, he thought.

He pulled off the dustsheet covering the car and climbed into the narrow, brown leather bucket driver's seat. Holding the four-spoked, wood-rimmed steering wheel in his right hand, he took a great gulp from the whiskey bottle. He felt the coarse, fiery liquid flowing down his throat and into his stomach. It sent calming signals to his brain and a second large gulp made him drift away.

I'm rushing downhill past the pits at Spa Francorchamps. The strong, super-charged engine in the Bugatti Type 35 urges me towards the left-hand bend at the bottom of the hill. Sweeping through the left-hander and braking hard, the firm brake pedal gives me confidence as I go down to second gear and slow into the right-hand l'Ancienne Douane hairpin. The backend of the little car kicks out, trying to spin me round. With a quick left flick of the wood-rimmed steering wheel, I am accelerating hard out of the hairpin. Now I am climbing steeply uphill onto the long straight. Picking up speed, I am drifting through the left-hand sweep at the top of the hill. I start plunging downhill, 4th gear flat out. The rev counter reads 5,300 as I flash past the houses at Burnenvillie, and then the left and right curves of Malmedy. They are already behind me. 'Get ready,' I tell myself, the Masta kink is ahead.

'Keep your right foot hard down,' my heart says, but my brain says, 'lift it, you stupid bugger'. I ignore that and phew, we're through. The Bugatti is kicking up dust at the edge of the road. The exhilaration, the rushing wind, the flies peppering my face, the sweet, singing, super-charged engine. I'm on full power all the way down to Stavelot, the tight, right-hand bend. The straight cut gears are engaging second gear as I press the sharp clutch. Braking hard now I feel the front wheels scrubbing sideways, protesting. I'm through, uphill again, building up speed all the time, gliding, almost floating, through the fast curves of La Carriere, my right foot flat to the floor. The fearsome Blanchimont approaches, and the narrow Bugatti tyres dance sideways as I turn into the first left bend too fast; it's over-steering! But a slight correction and all's well again. I drift gracefully through the second left-hand bend and touch the grass at the edge of the road. Flat out again to the left-hand kink and La Source hairpin is already upon us! Braking hard, I change down to first gear and kiss the grass, with the front right tyre at the apex.

Next door's cockerel bellowed a "cock-a-doodle-doo", an early morning announcement of territory. Frank woke with a start, for a moment unsure of where he was. Then the pain in his knee left him in no doubt. He was still wedged in the driver's seat of the Bugatti. On the passenger seat he noticed an empty bottle of whiskey on its side. The remains of its contents were puddled on the brown leather seat. He painfully extracted himself from the vehicle and unbolted the workshop door. A dull, dawn light and the hard, sharp air made him decide to walk off his aches, pains and hangover with a trip to his place, the Devil's Ditch.

An hour later, a refreshed Frank walked back into the yard. He could smell the toast and hear the noise of his young daughters laughing as they ate their breakfast in the kitchen and got ready for school.

Suddenly somehow, the future didn't seem quite so bleak. A swift wash in the cold water from the outside pump sharpened him up, and Frank hobbled into the house to face his wife and another day.

23

The inquest had been set for 20th September three weeks after the accident. It was to be held at the Coroner's Court in Weybridge. The day after the accident, the Cartland family had been deemed newsworthy again. Once more journalists commandeered the Red Lion pub, with their constant questions making life difficult for the villagers of Burlham.

Two days before the inquest, Mary came home from school early.

"What's the matter, why have you come home?" Margaret asked her when Mary stomped into the house.

"Billy Knowles said that my dad is a killer, just like his brother, so I punched him in the face," said Mary. "Then that old witch, Miss Manners, sent me home."

"Oh, Mary, you can't go around hitting people. I hope you have said you're sorry?" said Margaret.

"I'm not sorry, I'd hit him again, or anyone else, that said that about my dad," Mary replied.

"Go to your room this minute, I've had enough of all this," shouted Margaret, pushing her towards the stairs. Margaret's nerves were shot. Even though Doctor Jones had given her some sedatives, she felt unable to cope with even more stress.

Mary stamped up to her room and slammed the door. The moment Frank came in from the workshop Margaret demanded

"Your daughter has been hitting people I want you to go up there and punish her."

Going to Mary's room, Frank knocked on the door and went in. But Mary wasn't there, and her bedroom window was wide open. The little monkey has shimmied down the drainpipe, he smiled to himself.

Margaret had followed Frank up to the room. She didn't trust him to be firm with their daughter.

"Where is she?" she asked, with a hysterical pitch to her voice.

"Don't worry, I'll find her," said Frank.

"This is all your fault as usual". Frank knew what the next sentenced would be.

"Your bloody motors will be the death of us all," Margaret added as she pushed Frank out of the front door.

"Don't you dare come back until you've found her." Frank had those words ringing in his ears as he hurried down the cottage path. He had a good idea where Mary had gone, as her favorite bike was missing. Frank jumped on his bicycle, which had been motorised since his Isle of Man accident.

Now the smoking, noisy little engine on the bike propelled him off to the Devil's Dyke.

He expected to find Mary in the hiding place in the gorse bushes at the top of the dyke. These were the same bushes he had always escaped to when life became too difficult. He had shown her the secret place when they had been on one of the long, slow walks together. Sure enough, he saw Mary's bike lying on its side on the slope of the dyke. Mary was not surprised to see him.

"Why does everyone hate us and call you a killer?" she said as he sat down next to her. "I just want all those horrid people to disappear and leave us alone."

"You mustn't worry about other people. Most of them are just jealous and they like seeing people like us in trouble," said Frank. "I'm really proud of you standing up for me, but you really shouldn't go around hitting people."

As he spoke, Frank kissed the tight, black curls on the top of Mary's head. He put his arm around her and gave her a strong hug.

But despite the reassurances he gave to his daughter, Frank knew he was a murderer. He had never told anyone about how he had shot that poor French boy in the war.

He had managed to put that horror to the back of his mind, but right now the memory of it seemed very raw.

They sat there for five minutes without a word, comfortable together, before Mary said.

"Dad, are you ever worried or scared of anything?" Frank thought for a moment before replying.

"No, I don't think that I have ever been scared, but since you came along I do worry about you. I just want you to have a happy life."

Mary noticed tears in her father's eyes.

"You don't need to worry about me." She said with a weak smile. "I'm Fearless Frank's daughter, remember?"

"You sure are," he said, hugging her tight. "Now let's go back home and face someone who is really, really scary…your mother."

Mary giggled and gave him a long kiss on the cheek.

Frank didn't sleep at all the night before the inquest. It wasn't Margaret's light rhythmic snores that kept him awake. In fact, he found them rather comforting, as they reminded him of a distant motorcycle engine echoing through the mountains of the Isle of Man.

With the grey, early morning light creeping along the bedroom ceiling, he wondered how he had gotten himself into such a mess. *Why does life start out so simple and suddenly become so complicated?* he wondered. Feeling sorry for himself, he suddenly envied his old school mates who had been content to stay in the village and just work the land all their lives.

Bloody cars, bloody motorbikes, bloody engines, he thought. I wish they had never been invented. At least George Marshall had achieved his ambition, even if it did kill him. All I've got is a ruined knee to remind me of my failure.

The sudden sound of Emily crying for her mother brought him back to reality. Frank knew that he had a very difficult and emotional day ahead.

The high-profile event was of international interest, the world's press had crammed themselves into the courtroom. Following the accident, sensationalist headlines covered the front pages of all the newspapers

"Lord Marshall's son killed at Brooklands - member of a killer's family blamed," was just one of the Daily Mirror headlines.

Extensive coverage had been given to George's death, and some populist papers even showed a grainy, black, and white photograph of his body as it lay on the track. In contrast, the deaths of Albert and Madge Smith were given just a couple of sentences. They were nothing but a footnote at the end of each report.

Albert and Madge Smith (Albert had not officially changed their name to Smyth, so legally they were still called Smith) had not been blessed with children. At the inquest, their four parents sat quietly alone in one corner. The Marshalls were there in force, of course. Silvia was sitting slightly apart, as if to distance herself from the rest. Frank thought that Silvia looked very pale and drawn; while he knew that the fixed scowl on the face of Victoria Marshall meant she had an overwhelming desire to see him officially blamed for the accident.

Frank was called up first.

"Can you give us your explanation of the accident that caused the deaths of the Honorable George Marshall, Albert Smith and Madge Smith?" said the coroner after Frank had been sworn in.

"Yes, sir, I had advised George Marshall that changing the axle ratio on his car would cause the engine to over rev and…"

"What's over rev?" interrupted the coroner.

"Revs is short for revolutions per minute, sir. All engines have a safe limit," said Frank quietly.

"Thank you, carry on, Mr. Cartland."

"Mr. Marshall then ignored my warning and told his mechanics to change it. That is the reason the engine blew up, which then caused the accident."

Frank felt rather overawed by the experience, with the hostile Marshalls staring at him. They had made sure that all their influential friends, and the press, knew that they thought George's death was completely Frank's fault.

"Did anyone hear you give that warning to George Marshall?" asked the coroner.

"Yes, sir, his three mechanics were standing next to the car and heard everything, but they had to do whatever George Marshall told them."

"Thank you, Mr. Cartland, you may stand down," said the coroner.

Frank quickly went back to his seat and Margaret gave him a weak smile.

It was unfortunate that the three mechanics had been the only witnesses to the argument Frank had with George about the dangers of changing the axle ratio.

Freddie O'Hare and two other well-known Brooklands drivers then gave their evidence. They all confirmed that Frank was an exceptional engine builder and could not be held responsible for the disaster.

"Everyone knows that he's the best bloody engine builder at Brooklands," said Freddie in his usual colourful way.

"So, anyone who blames Frank for this accident is talking out of their arse. I saw the smoke coming from Marshall's car on that last lap, the bloody fool should have lifted his foot."

In fact, Freddie had been standing half a mile away and could not have noticed the smoke, but he thought that might help Frank.

"George Marshall couldn't drive a racing car to save his life," he added, rather unfortunately.

Next, the coroner called the three Marshall mechanics in turn. Under oath, each said that although they were close by, as Frank Cartland had said. When Mr. Marshall came back after his practice run, they had not heard the warning Frank had given to their boss.

"They are all lying, she's put them up to this," Frank interrupted. He stood up and pointed at Victoria Marshall, as the third mechanic nervously confirmed that they had heard nothing.

"Sit down and keep quiet," the coroner told Frank sharply.

Before the hearing Victoria Marshall had, as Frank guessed, instructed the mechanics to say they didn't hear the argument. They were all employed on the family estate and couldn't afford to lose their jobs. The promise of some additional cash made certain that they would do as she insisted.

With no more witnesses to call the coroner adjourned the court while he considered his verdict.

A worried Frank knew that it was going to be his word against a dead man and, although other drivers were there to support him, he feared the worst.

After the adjournment and a very long hour's wait for Frank, they were all called back into the courtroom. With the room in complete silence, the coroner stood up.

"Having considered all the available evidence I can only conclude that this tragic event was an unfortunate accident," he said.

"Therefore, the verdict of this court for all three fatalities is death by misadventure."

It was a great relief to Frank and his supporters. He pushed through the crowd of reporters and left the courtroom with a tearful Margaret by his side. Lady Victoria Marshall rushed over to him and, almost spitting into his face, said,

"Cartland, you haven't heard the end of this. We will make sure your life is a misery from now on."

With Margaret sobbing, the shouts of the Marshalls and the world's press in his ears, Frank hurried to his old Morris 8 and drove slowly back to his Cambridgeshire home.

Before leaving for the inquest, Margaret had informed Frank that she was expecting their fourth child. While back in Sefton Manor, Silvia Marshall had told no one that she was also pregnant.

The funeral of George William Marshall was a very quiet affair. There was none of the pomp and ceremony that had accompanied the funeral of his two brothers. After a private service in the family church, George was placed in the Marshall family crypt in Chichester cemetery, next to the remains of his brothers, Stuart, and Matthew.
On the coffin lid, Silvia had insisted that George's Brooklands 120mph badge should be inset into the oak, alongside the Marshall coat of arms.
Lord John Marshall and Lady Victoria Marshall looked a pitiful pair as they stood in silence inside the mausoleum. They had now lost all their children. The newspapers the next day were full of pictures of the grieving widow Silvia, who was looking stunning, if slightly overweight, in black.

The only two people who'd had some affection for George, his chauffeur James Bird and his lover Hellen Dupery did not attend the funeral.
Hellen had deliberately stayed away from Brooklands on the day of George's record attempt. She knew that the sporting press would be more interested in the reactions of Silvia and her than to give any praise for George's efforts. She didn't want to take his moment of glory away from him.
Hellen heard the news of the accident in London that night when she read the headlines in the Evening Standard, she was genuinely upset, although it felt more like losing a faithful old dog than a soul mate.

Like Silvia, she knew that George was out of his depth and did feel some remorse that she had, in some way, contributed to his death. But his death gave her the opportunity to move on, something she had already decided she would have to do.

To that end, only two days before the record attempt, she had made plans to take up the offer of a lover, Brooklands racing driver, Baron von Rosenberg. He had invited her stay at his castle in the Black Forest, only ten miles from the famous Nurburgring racetrack. She had decided that if the chance arose she would stay in Germany.
Hellen had called into Frank's workshop earlier that day to give him the news. The well-used, and now rather battered, blue Bugatti sat alone and dusty at the back of the workshop.

"I am going away to Germany, Frankie, I don't think I will be racing Bleu Bebe again," she said.

"Very sorry to see you go, Miss Hellen," said Frank, "What shall I do with this pile of unpaid bills of yours I've got in the draw. I've been working on the old Bugatti these last two years and you haven't paid me a bean."

Hellen gave Frank one of her famous big, warm smiles, as she always did when he asked for some payment.

"Oh, Frankie, I'm sorry, I have no money now…but, I know, why don't you take Bleu Bebe as payment. She's yours to keep."

"Not sure she's worth much," said Frank, scratching his head. "But I've grown fond of the old girl…so you've got a deal."

"Wonderful! I know she is in safe hands," exclaimed a happy Hellen, clapping her hands together. Hellen gave her faithful Bugatti a final pat, and Frank a long, soft kiss on the cheek, then she turned and glided out of the workshop, without a backward glance. That was the last time Frank ever saw Hellen Dupery.

James Bird had worked for the Marshall family all his life. His father had been head coachman, and when he had become too frail to carry on, James took over the post. Social pressures ensured that all the major families had motorised transport as soon as they became reasonably reliable and the Marshalls were no exception. Their first car had arrived in April 1902. James was their chauffeur from that day on.
James had soon become an expert at curing the many mechanical ills of those early temperamental vehicles. All the Marshall family transport became his responsibility, from that first Panhard et Levassor touring car, to the final second-hand Bentley.

When George had shown a real interest in driving and motors, unlike anyone else in the family, James had encouraged his hobby. On the day of George's death, James was back at Sefton Manor trying to repair the old Bentley, which had broken down once again.
Local reporters descended on the manor with news of George's death long before the Marshall family arrived home. James was careful not to speak to them, but knowing George as he did, he was not very surprised to learn that he had been killed.

He blamed Silvia, whom he hated for the way she had controlled and belittled George in recent years, just like his mother before her. Of course, he didn't share those thoughts with anyone

24

On a cool March morning in 1934, in their bedroom at Ivy Cottage, Margaret gave birth to a 6lbs 2oz healthy boy with black curly hair. They named their new arrival Peter Joseph Cartland.

Just 20 hours later, in a private room at Chichester General Hospital in Sussex, Silvia Marshall gave birth to a healthy, black-haired boy of a very similar weight to Peter Cartland.

Of course, Lady Victoria Marshall was delighted to have another boy in the family, even though for generations all other Marshall boys had had blond hair. Anyway, she still had her blond-haired oldest grandson William to mold. He would carry on the family traditions and preserve the Marshall name.

Silvia was certain the father of her new son was not her late husband George - they hadn't had sex for at least two years before his death.

In fact, as soon as she knew she was pregnant, Silvia worked out that Frank Cartland was most likely the father. When she saw her new son's dark curly hair for the first time she was certain of it. *I only went to give him a present, didn't expect one myself,* she thought with some amusement.

Her new son was named David William Marshall, with the blessing of Victoria Marshall. Not that it mattered to Silvia what her mother-in-law thought. She was by now a very wealthy woman in her own right. She laughed to herself regarding the irony of it. She was now far wealthier than the snobbish older Marshalls.

Her father, with whom she had never been close, had died of heart failure, just a year after his grandson William was born. Simon Moncrieff left half of his fortune and the factories to his sons. He left the rest, including their three houses, to Silvia's mother.

Alice Moncrieff had not lived long to spend and enjoy the money. Sadly, she committed suicide in 1927. The preceding years had not been kind to her. With the marriage of Silvia to George Marshall, she had naively expected to be accepted into the Marshall social scene.

She imagined being seen at Ascot, Wimbledon and Henley in the summer, going skiing in Switzerland for Christmas, then spending three months in the South of France until England warmed again in spring.

But having an old family background was more important to the Marshalls, especially to Victoria, than possessing a wealthy or notorious family history. Also, coming from the north meant that Alice had no chance of joining in these traditional pleasures with the old families.

Once Victoria Marshall had achieved her aim of marrying the family back into money, she had no time for Alice Moncrieff. Her forceful nature ensured that none of her social scene welcomed Alice either.

Disappointed and bored, Alice took many young lovers, both before and after Simon died. In a social whirl of parties, drink, and drugs, she was quickly losing her looks and her health. She contracted syphilis when she reached forty but was in complete denial about the infection until it was far too late.

Silvia had very little contact with her mother during this period. Alice's erratic behaviour and many young lovers had become an embarrassment to her daughter. When she eventually found out about her mother's condition Alice was already on the edge of madness.

Silvia arranged for her to be sent to a private nursing home in Eastbourne, hoping for some cure.

It had been a year since the christening of William, when she had last seen her mother, she eased her guilt by arranging a visit.

With great shock, Silvia looked at this once-beautiful woman and realised that the treatment wasn't working.

"How are you, Mother?" Silvia said, trying not to show how upset she was feeling.

Grabbing her arm and digging her nails painfully into her daughter's arm, Alice screamed into her face.

"Take me home from here, take me home, they are all trying to kill me."

Silvia pulled away and a doctor rushed in to sedate poor Alice.

Three purple bruises were already appearing on her right forearm, as Silvia left the nursing home, knowing she would never visit her mother again.

One month later, on a cold and windy September morning, Alice walked out of the nursing home unnoticed by the staff. She found her way to Beachy Head and, according to a dog-walking witness, walked off the cliffs.

It was five days before Alice's body washed ashore. She was found two miles along the coast from the famous landmark. Although the mortuary assistant had done his best before Silvia went to identify the body, some of the effects of five days of being bashed by rocks and considered fodder by crabs and small fish were still visible. The soft tissues and the eyes were the first to go, but thankfully Alice's eyelids were closed.

Her mother's death had a large impact on Silvia, although she felt more relief than sadness as she stood looking down at the white, sad shell. Silvia knew that she owed this woman a great deal of thanks. Without her mother's ambition and forcefulness, she would probably have ended up being married to an uncouth Northern lout, instead of now being one of the richest women in England.
Silvia had to organise the funeral herself and soon accepted how few real friends her mother had. Only eight people attended when Alice was buried in her hometown cemetery in Wakefield on a grey October day.
None of the Marshall family attended the funeral.

25

In Sussex, William Marshall had grown into a strapping, handsome and self-confident young man. Although he had the blond Marshall hair, his high cheekbones and strong brown eyes were inherited from his mother.

The traumatic death of his father, which he had witnessed as a young boy, had no lasting effect on him. He had seen the lack of affection between his mother and father as he was growing up.

Just as George had been shown no love from his father, George had never demonstrated much love for William. Even so, bearing witness to their father's death would have a long-lasting effect on many young boys, but William was made of sterner stuff.

Her sons' lack of emotional reaction did surprise his mother, but she was proud of, rather than worried by, his apparent detachment. William did not attend the inquest, although he had heard all the gossip at Sefton Manor. He knew his father had not received much respect from the staff. The day before the inquest, William found James alone in one of the garages and went in to talk to him.

"Tell me, what do you think happened to my father at Brooklands, James?" he asked.

"Sorry, Master William, but I didn't see the accident. I was here repairing the old Bentley," said James.

"But you did know my father well, so you must have some idea why he crashed. Most of the family are sure it was Frank Cartland's fault."

"Your father was desperate to get his 120mph badge, so I'm sure he was trying very hard," said James diplomatically. "Now, please excuse me, Lord John wants the car to take him to the station."

With great relief James escaped further questioning from William. He didn't want his true thoughts to be known. He had gotten to know George's nature quite well over the years. He felt sorry for him and was convinced that George would have brought the accident on himself.

After the inquest, William's grandmother Victoria had turned her attentions to him. When her twin sons had been killed in the war her indifference towards her only remaining son George had changed. She had devoted her energies to finding him a wife. Now she intended to take full control of William's life.

"You hold full responsibility for the future of the thousand-year Marshall dynasty, William," she had said when he reached the age of sixteen.

"I intend to help you fulfill your obligations." Despite his relative youth, William made it clear that he was not ready to be told how to run his life. Unlike his father, he was his own man.

"I know you mean well, grandmother," he said, "I do understand that when grandfather dies I will be the eldest male Marshall, but I intend to make my own mind up regarding what I do."

A shocked Victoria had no response. No one had dared to question her plans before.

Silvia was delighted to see William stand up to the old woman. She was proud of the fact he had a mind of his own, unlike his late father.

William had also inherited her passion for fast, mechanical things, much to his grandmother's dismay. She was horrified when she found out that he had attended several Brooklands race meetings since his father had been killed. To make matters worse, William had fallen in love with the fascinating flying machines stationed and built there and preferred airplanes to racing cars.

"Next week I will have my first flying lesson," William proudly announced to his mother as they drove home from the autumn members' meeting.

"Well, don't tell your grandmother," said Silvia, "she is paranoid about your safety. She would keep you in a glass case if she could.
"

William started his flying lessons in a Tiger Moth at the Brooklands track, and soon proved to have a natural ability. By the following spring he had obtained his flying license. He called at Sefton Manor on his way home.

"Good evening, grandmother," he said as he gave Victoria a perfunctory kiss on the cheek. "I thought you would like to know that I have just obtained my pilot's license. I intend to join the Royal Air Force next year."

"Why didn't you tell me you were flying? … it's … it's so dangerous"

"I didn't want to worry you or grandfather, so I decided to wait until I had qualified."

"You are due to go up to Oxford next year, so I will not allow you to join," said a now very red-faced Victoria. There was an uneasy silence.

"Well, now I must go and give mother the news," said William. "I thought you would be pleased that I told you first." William went back out to his motorbike and rode the quarter of a mile down the drive to his home at the lodge. He was determined to join the RAF as soon as possible, despite his grandmother's protests.

26

Four years had passed since the death of George Marshall. These had been largely uninspiring for Frank Cartland, but they were quiet and happy for his family.

Having no knowledge of his other new son David, Frank spent most of his time running the garage and enjoying time with his growing children, much to Margaret's satisfaction. By now she had resigned herself to Mary remaining more interested in oil than perfume. *At least the other two are proper girls*, she thought

It made her smile to know that the Marshalls had used their influence and money to make sure that Frank was unwelcome at Brooklands, and almost anywhere else where motor racing took place. He had once again been given back to her.

Frank regretted having missed much of his older children's early years, and he wanted to be around as Peter grew up. But unfortunately for Margaret, no matter how much Frank wanted to be a normal family man, he still had a stronger force inside him bubbling to be let out once again.

On an early April morning, Doctor Howard Jones turned up at the garage. He hastily stopped, got out of his Morris 8 and rushed into the workshop brandishing a newspaper.

"It's all in here, you're cleared at last," he said excitedly to a surprised Frank.

"Slow down, Howard, what are you talking about?"

"Look what one of the old Marshall mechanics has said to the papers. He did hear you warning his boss about changing the axle ratio."

"But why say that after all this time?"

"Don't know, but he has - see for yourself," said Howard, handing Frank the paper.
Sure enough, there on the back page of the Daily Mirror, Frank read the headline.

"Marshall mechanics lied at Brooklands inquest.Alfie Barnes, chief mechanic to George Marshall on the day he was killed at Brooklands, now admits that he did hear the famous engine builder Frank Cartland warn his boss that changing the axle would be dangerous," read the article. "None of the Marshall family was available for comment." It ended.

"That's all?" said Frank, throwing the paper down.
"The damage is already done… it won't change anything now."
But inside he did feel a flutter of excitement. The racing passion was still burning deep within him.

On a beautiful, cloudless, late October day later that year, Frank packed the family into an old Austin 10 he had recently rebuilt. They drove the 3 miles up to Newmarket Heath for a picnic, and to watch the final horseraces of the season.
Sitting on a blanket on the lush green turf, with the skylarks singing and the hooves of the racehorses sounding like distant thunder, Frank reflected that although he had come a long way in 38 years, he was almost back where he had started. Sometimes he could almost feel those sharp cobbles digging into his body as his father beat him all those years ago.

He watched his three girls laughing and shouting as they ran up and down the green slopes of the Devil's Dyke, just as he and Joe used to do.

They were chasing their little wire-haired Terrier dog, Cassie, granddaughter of his old friend, Spike.

Mary had certainly inherited Frank's love for speed. Still a tomboy, she was more interested, to Frank's joy, in cars and engines than boys, and spent many happy hours with him in the workshop.

Now a lovely 18-year-old, she was completely unaware of the effect her looks had on all the local lads.

With Emily and Edith, both much more like their mother than him, chasing after their older sister, Frank was, at that moment, contented. He thought how his life as it was now should be enough.

Looking down into the smiling, wide brown eyes of the four-year-old boy playing with the little tin car Frank had made him, he thought, just maybe, Peter could be the champion racing driver in the Cartland family. This was the one ambition that had eluded him.

They were all happy when they drove home that afternoon, but Margaret's mood changed the moment the garage came into view. Until now she had been very content. Her life was finally settled, she had her family all around her. She wanted nothing more. But her contentment was about to end.

Waiting outside the garage was Freddie O'Hare. He was leaning against a sleek black racing MG Magnette K3. Pete Betts was admiring the car and filling petrol into it from one of Frank's yellow Shell petrol pumps.

That bastard, he always brings trouble, thought Margaret as soon as she saw who it was. With a brief, wary "hello" to Margaret, Freddie then said to Frank,

"I'm on my way to Donington Park to watch these new German racing cars perform. I thought you would like to come with me?"

Of course, Frank had been reading all about the German Mercedes and Auto Union cars in his monthly bible Speed magazine.

He knew that they were now dominating Grand Prix motor racing. The race at Donington had been due to run earlier in the year, but it had been cancelled owing to the uncertain political situation in Europe.

Recently, the British Prime Minister, Neville Chamberlain, had come back from meeting Adolf Hitler in Germany. All the papers were full of the headline "Peace in our Time," and photographs of Chamberlain waving a piece of paper they had both signed.

The International Donington Grand Prix race had been rescheduled for the next weekend, on 22nd October.

Frank also knew that Chancellor Hitler had invested millions of Deutsche Marks in the German racing teams. The chance to see these incredible machines was something he couldn't miss.

"Just give me a minute, Freddie," he said, as his family got out of the car and went into the cottage.

He followed Margaret, who had stormed into the kitchen, and took hold of her arm, forcing her to turn and face him. He looked pleadingly at her with his bright, excited eyes. He was just like a little puppy begging for food.

"Do you mind if I go with him?" he asked.

"Of course, I mind, you bloody fool," Margaret snapped, "but I know you are going to go anyway, so why don't you just bugger off!"

Frank tried to give her a peck on the cheek, but she turned away from him. He went into their bedroom, grabbed a clean pair of socks, some pants, and a shirt, then stuffed them into his old, brown leather travel bag. Mary was standing at the cottage door blocking his way

"I want to come with you."

"I'm sorry, Speedy," Frank replied, using his nickname for her. "I really need you here to look after the garage. Oh, and your mother and sisters," he added. Seeing the tears in her eyes, he said,

"You know I love you, Mary," before giving her a quick hug.

Then he slipped into the passenger seat of the black MG. Freddie dropped the clutch, Frank turned and shouted back to Mary.

"I promise I'll take you next year."

But Mary didn't hear his shout. The roar from the MG exhaust had drowned out his words.

Freddie and Frank happily disappeared up the road to Donington Park, once again they quickly left the mundane real world behind them.

Watching until the noise of the MG had become just the sound of a distant angry bee, Mary turned and stomped back into the cottage.

Her younger sisters and little brother were happily playing some make-believe game around the kitchen table. Mary realised that she had never been as content as they were. Thinking of her father, she whispered to herself, *I'm going to be just as selfish as you as soon as I get the chance. Let's see if you like that.*

Hearing Mary come back into the kitchen, Margaret shouted down from her bedroom,

"Mary, be a dear and make me a cup of tea. I'm having a lie down, I've got another headache."

27

Frank had been wrong about the newspaper revelations. Alfie Barnes' change of tune certainly affected the Marshalls. Barnes had been dismissed by Victoria Marshall as part of the family's cost-cutting exercise and became very bitter when they evicted him from his cottage on the estate. The twenty pounds the Daily Mirror gave him for the story didn't last very long though. Drink had always been Alfie's weakness.

Victoria stormed around the manor the day the story was printed, ensuring the staff said nothing to the ten pressmen standing at the gates.

"If anyone approaches you, make sure you all say that Barnes was a drunken liar," she told them. "If I hear of anyone saying anything different they will be fired."

William, of course, still wanted to know what had happened, but no one, not even his mother, would talk about it.

On one of his visits to Brooklands flying club, William had called at one of the sheds used by Freddie O'Hare. Nervously he approached Freddie,

"Excuse me, Mr. O'Hare, but could you tell me where Frank Cartland has his garage?" Freddie recognised this tall blond lad standing in front of him, and he was very surprised by his politeness.

"Why should I tell you. Don't want you causing any more trouble for him," said Freddie, giving William a threatening look. "Your fucking family has done enough damage to his life. They got him thrown out of here."

"I just want to know what really happened that day when my father died," said William, looking Freddie straight in the eye.

Freddie was impressed with this lad. He's much more his mother's son than his father's, he thought.

"If I do give you his address, and I then find out that you caused that family more misery, I'll be after you," said Freddie.

"I give you my word. I've no intention of causing any trouble," replied William.

As Freddie gave William the address of Ivy Garage, he added,   "Anyway, I can save you the trouble of speaking to Frank Cartland. Your old man died because he was a crap racing driver - it was no fault of Frank's."

William went home that evening and spoke to his mother.

"I intend to go and see Frank Cartland next week," he said.

"I'm not sure that's a good idea, but I will not try to stop you," said a surprised Silvia, "You can't change what has happened."

"I know that, but I would like to hear what he has to say. No one here will speak to me about the crash that killed father. Grandmother forbids the servants, and they are all afraid of her."

"It's also because we just want to forget about it," Silvia argued.

"Well, I'm going to listen to his version of the accident," said William determinedly.

Silvia, with some excitement, suddenly knew that the older generations of Marshalls were gradually losing their influence. The actions of her son were going to ensure that.

The old Marshalls were fading away. They were growing old and crumbling - just like Sefton Manor, which was proving far too expensive for Lord Marshall to maintain.

In the last year he'd had to close the west wing of the house. There was no Marshall money left for the necessary repairs. Dry rot had spread throughout this wing of the house, and the roof leaked in many places. The reducing Marshall fortune forced Lord John to slash the manor staff considerably over the preceding five years.
Only six servants remained to tend to his and Lady Victoria's needs, one being the faithful old chauffeur James, although he now drove them slowly in an old and well-used Bentley. The family Silver Ghost was just a distant memory for James. It had been sold long ago, back in 1925.

After the inquest, the older Marshall clan had ostracised Silvia. Victoria was extremely bitter that Frank Cartland had escaped blame for the accident and her son's death at Brooklands. She really needed someone to be culpable.
She made sure that the older Marshalls considered Silvia as guilty as Frank Cartland, for forcing her son into taking the risks that killed him.
What Victoria and the rest thought did not matter in the least to Silvia. She had William and now her younger son, David.
She was certain that the older Marshalls would be long dead before they could get their claws into David. She was confident that she and her boys would be the dominating forces in the Marshall family in the future.

The day after her father had left for Donington, Mary was pottering in the workshop feeling miserable. She was still angry with him for not taking her with him.

Six months earlier he had been putting oil in the bores and turning over the engine of the Bugatti Type 35. Mary remembered hearing her mother's sharp words when she first noticed the Bugatti.

"What have you brought that old thing here for?" Her angry words when she found out that her dad had taken the Bugatti instead of payment from Hellen Dupery for all the work he had done.

"You are so stupid, Frank Cartland," she had shouted. "We need money not that horrible, worthless, blue piece of junk."

Frank had ignored her harsh remarks, as he usually did these days. Mary knew he loved the car, and she could see why. With its beautiful shape, its distinctive alloy wheels and the superb engineering of its mechanical parts, it was a work of art. Mary knew he intended to keep it, even though it was now it would be uncompetitive against more modern cars. While he had been turning over the Bugatti engine, Frank had noticed his long-forgotten Triumph motorcycle under an old sheet in the corner *This is just the thing for Mary*, he had thought. Her father had wheeled a rusty and dusty old motorbike out into the yard.

"This is my old faithful Triumph, it hasn't been used for years, but if you can get it going it's yours," Frank had said to her.

"Thanks, Dad, I'll soon have it sorted and running like new. That old motorised bike is far too slow for me now, and anyway, it's always bloody well breaking down."

"Don't swear, you know your mother wouldn't like it," was all Frank had said.

Mary was remembering her boast as she struggled to remove the oily, old engine from the frame of the Triumph. The old nuts and bolts, which had rusted in place over the years were giving her problems. *This job is hard work*, she thought.
Suddenly, the spanner slipped, she smashed her hand hard onto the rough frame of the bike.

"Bugger!" she exclaimed as blood flowed from her skinned knuckles and cut finger. She was sucking her finger, trying to stop the flow, when she heard the deep, throaty sound of a powerful motorbike nearby. Forgetting her damaged hand, she ran outside.

"Wow," she said as the magnificent machine stopped in front of the petrol pumps.
The rider, still with his helmet and goggles on, sat astride the bike looking straight at her. He got off the bike ansd slowly removed his helmet and goggles. Mary saw before her a tall, strong-featured young man with unfashionable, long blond hair.

William Marshall had been intending to make this visit to Frank Cartland for a long time. Now that he was finally here he was very nervous.
He had not expected to find a beautiful young girl in oil-stained overalls at Frank's garage.

"Hello," he said quietly.

"Is this your bike?" asked Mary excitedly. She looked over the machine with envious eyes.

"Ye … Yes it is," said William, unable to take his eyes off this unusual, lovely girl.

"I would like to speak to Frank Cartland. Is this his garage?"

Mary, still studying the motorbike, did not appear to hear him.

"It's a Brough Superior, isn't it? Which model?"

Like her father before her, Mary spent hours studying motor and motorcycling magazines. She knew that this was the "Rolls-Royce" of motorbikes, and that one had recently broken the lap record at Brooklands, averaging more than 120mph. She remembered because her dad had said at the time,

"That guy must be brave. George Marshall couldn't even drive his car as quick as that."

Surprised at her knowledge, William replied,

"Yes, it's a SS680 overhead valve, V twin."

"I love it," she said, looking up at him for the first time. For a few seconds their eyes locked. Mary broke the moment

"Sor...sorry, who did you say you are?"

"I'm William Marshall. I am looking for Frank Cartland."

It was Mary's turn to be surprised, and her happy mood immediately turned to anger.

"He's not here, and even if he was he wouldn't want to see or speak to you," she said sharply. "He's not going to be home for days, so you had better get back on that bloody machine and ride away from here."

Completely taken aback by her sudden change of mood, William said,

"I ... I just want to speak to him about my father, but I've got a letter here in case he wouldn't see me. I haven't come to cause any trouble."

William unzipped his brown leather jacket, pulled out an envelope and offered it to Mary.

"Would you please give this to him when he comes back?"

William stood with his arm outstretched. Mary, hands on hips and legs slightly apart, had moved ten feet further away from him. Slowly, William stepped towards her, arm still outstretched, offering the envelope.

Silently Mary snatched the letter from his hand. Spots of her blood sprayed onto the envelope and the sleeve of Williams's leather jacket.

William gave her a weak smile and turned back to the Brough. He put his helmet back on, pulled down his goggles and kick-started the bike. The deep, base sound as it burst into life caused Mary's knees to buckle. She held onto one of the pumps for support.

A very confused Mary watched the Brough Superior disappear down the lane. But it wasn't just the bike that had affected her. Her mother had filled her and her younger sisters' heads with stories over the years. She had bitterly told them how the Marshall family was made up of evil, nasty, rich people, and that they had ruined the Cartland family's lives. Mary, of course, remembered the accident that killed George Marshall, but whenever she asked her father what had happened, the scar on his forehead would turn pink. He would get angry and refuse to talk about it. *That young man did not seem nasty at all,* she thought. In fact, it was just the opposite. Meeting him produced emotions she had never experienced before.

Mary decided not to tell her mother about the visit from William Marshall. Fortunately, Margaret had taken the younger children to her father's bakery for some cakes. Mary went back into the small garage office, sat down at the old desk and wrapped an old rag around her cut hand. Then she opened the letter.

William never needed an excuse to ride his motorbike. The fact that Burlham was almost 200 miles from his Sussex home was no problem for him. With the Brough effortlessly eating the miles, he sped along the narrow, dusty lanes back south. He was lost in the sensation of pure joy that the bike gave him with its' speed and power. His heart was beating with the pulse of the V twin engine, and he felt like the bike and his body had merged into one living machine.

"Don't expect too much from him," Silvia had said that morning when he announced he was on his way to see Frank Cartland. "Since the inquest your grandmother has been making his life Hell."
On his return to the lodge that evening, Silvia was waiting for him. Hearing the Brough arrive home, she went out onto the gravel drive to greet him.

"What did Frank Cartland say to you?" she asked the moment her son took off his helmet.

"He wasn't there. I left a letter with a pretty, black-haired young woman in overalls."
Silvia immediately noticed the wistful look in her son's eyes.

"Who is the young woman?" she asked

"I didn't have time to find out, she got very angry when I told her who I was. She had been really interested in the Brough before I told her my name."
William's disappointment was obvious to his mother.

"That sounds like Frank's daughter, Mary. I saw her once at Brooklands when she was a young girl. She was always just like him, mad about motors and covered in oil".

"I wish I'd had a chance to talk to her properly. I've never met a girl like her before," said William. He glanced down at the two dark spots on the sleeve of his jacket
"I hope she gives him the letter."
Pushing the Brough into the stables, which had been converted to its garage, he added, "If I don't join the Royal Air Force I have been thinking about applying for Cambridge University, so I'll call up there again in a few weeks."

"Do you think that's a good idea? You know all the Marshalls have gone to Oxford University in the past. Your grandmother will be very upset if you go to Cambridge instead." said Silvia.

"Don't worry, I'm sure I can handle her," William replied.
Silvia couldn't help smiling. She knew when a man was smitten…so many men had chased her over the years.

28

The German cars were sensational. Frank had never seen anything like them before. Driving one of the Auto Union cars was his hero Silvio Bellini. Bellini was a small Italian racing driver who had started racing motorcycles around the same time as Frank.

They had met on the Isle of Man in 1925. After his accident in the TT race, Frank had received a letter from Bellini offering his best wishes for a "rapido recupero". They lost touch after that, but Frank followed Silvio's progress each month in his motoring magazines, Speed and The Motor.

By the 1930s, Bellini had developed into one of the best racing drivers in the world. Arriving in the Donington paddock, Frank noticed the orange jumper of his old Italian friend. He was talking to his German mechanics. Tentatively Frank went over and reintroduced himself.

"Hello Silvio, I'm not sure if you remember me from your old motorcycling days?"

"Se mi remember you, my old amico," said Bellini, in his broken English. Shaking Frank's hand vigorously he pulled on his red leather racing helmet to start practice

"Come see me tardi," he said. As he stepped into the cockpit of the great silver Auto Union, the car appeared to swallow him.

"Even the steering wheel looks bigger than him," said Freddie. "How the Hell does he manage to drive that thing?"

Silvio slammed the Auto Union into gear and fishtailed out onto the Donington Park circuit.

"Bloody amazing," said Freddie, impressed, "I didn't know you were friends with racing royalty fearless"

"I haven't spoken to him for years," said a smiling Frank. He was really chuffed that Silvio Bellini had remembered him.

Bellini set the fastest laps at the start of practice, but then, when driving flat out downhill through Hollywood bends, he was startled to find a large deer on the track, which he was unable to avoid.

The silver Auto Union unfortunately killed the deer instantly, and Bellini damaged his ribs in the impact. Frank found him in the medical tent after practice. A young nurse was winding bandages around his ribs.

"I thought those antlers were going to spear you," said Frank.

"Se, bloody stupido animale, mi have antlers un trofeo," laughed Silvio.

"Are you going to be fit enough to race tomorrow?" questioned Frank,

"Naturalmente e vincerò," said the little Italian.

It was a bright sunny morning when, along with 60,000 other spectators, Frank and Freddie excitedly sat down to watch the powerful and dramatic Silver Arrows. This was the name given to all the Mercedes and Auto Union cars. Both manufacturers had painted their magnificent machines bright silver.

There were four Mercedes and three Auto Unions on the grid. The rest of the cars were mainly outdated English machines, the ERA and Frazer Nash cars being the quickest. Unfortunately, the fastest English car was over five seconds a lap slower than any of the sleek German machines.

The Duke of Kent started the 80-lap race. When he dropped the Union Jack, Silvio Bellini, in his bright orange sweater and red leather helmet, immediately roared his Auto Union to the front. After 20 laps the charging Bellini had opened up a large lead.

"Sod it," said a disappointed Frank, the next time the car came past them. "It sounds like the engine is misfiring." Sure enough, Bellini slowed into the pits at the end of that lap for a change of plugs.

"He can't win now," said a disgusted Frank to Freddie as the silver Auto Union eventually flashed past them. Although the car was running strongly again, they had dropped down to fourth place. Frank and Freddie stood watching from the banking, just before the hairpin bend. Next lap Bellini flew past them with the car almost sideways.

"He is driving like a mad man," said Freddie. This made Frank smile, as coming from Freddie that comment was funny. Freddie was the maddest driver he had even seen.

Then, right in front of them, one of the English cars blew its engine, dropping oil all over the track.

"Must be one of your engines," joked Freddie, but before Frank had time to reply, Bellini arrived at full speed and hit the oil slick. In an instant, the silver Auto Union slid sideways, broadside across the grass, but somehow the little man managed to wrestle the great car back onto the track. There was loud spontaneous applause from the crowd. It was a moment that all the spectators would remember for the rest of their lives.

"That guy is superhuman," Frank said loudly.
All the spectators who were privileged to have witnessed
Bellini in action that day knew they would never forget his
uncanny skill. Setting the fastest lap time after time, Silvio
Bellini was unstoppable. He re-took the lead on lap 67.

To great celebrations, he went on to win - a magnificent
victory. With the world's press and well-wishers
surrounding him, Frank was unable to speak to his old
friend after the race, but he still thought what a wonderful
weekend it had been.
One thing that did disturb him, and many of the other
English spectators, however, was the complete domination
of the German machines.

Frank remembered reading about the German Mercedes
team going in force to the 1914 French Grand Prix. They
finished first, second and third, just as the German cars at
the Donington Grand Prix had now dominated this race. A
few months after the 1914 French Grand Prix, Germany
was at war with France and England.

Driving back, a strangely subdued Freddie said,
        "Bloody hell, Fearless, how are we going to build cars
that can compete with those German monsters?"
Frank had no answer.
Late that Sunday evening, Freddie dropped Frank off at
home. Frank stood outside his garage for a long time after
the snarling MG had disappeared. He smoked a final
Woodbine as he leaned against one of his Shell petrol
pumps. With his ears still ringing from the shattering noise
of the V12 German engines, he knew he needed to be

immersed, once again, in the exciting, intoxicating world of motor racing.

He couldn't help it. Speed was in his blood.

It was 1938 and events in Europe were already taking the world on a terrifying, unstoppable course. Frank Cartland and Silvia Marshall had no idea that the consequences of these events would ensure that they would have little control over their own, or their family's futures.

Bibliography

Adventurers Fen : E.A.R.Ennion

Brooklands to Goodwood ; Rodney Walkerley

Brooklands Volume 1 W.Boddy

Bugatti Queen : Miranda Seymour

Early one Morning : Robert Ryan

Fast Women : John Bullock

My Lifetime in Motorsport : Sammy Davies

Norton Motor Cycles : Jim Reynolds

The British at Le Mans : Ian Wagstaff

The Donington Grand Prix : Dave Fern

The History of Motor Racing : W. Boddy

The Le Mans 24 Hours : David Hodges

The Roaring Twenties : Cyril Posthumus

The Story of the T.T : G.S.Davison

Pre-view
A Fatal Addiction

Part 2
The Triumphs and the Tragedies

Frank climbed onto the huge pile of rubble that had been
his cottage and began to lift the broken beams. "Pull, Pull,
Pull, Peter" shouted Frank to Peter who was already trying
to help. They were desperately choking in the cloying dust
that was rising from the chalky rubble. For hours they all
continued lifting the rubble and crushed beams, but there
was still no sign of his wife or daughter.
The German Doodlebug had arrived over Burlham at 10.45
that morning. Gravedigger Harry Williams dropped his
spade and looked up when he heard the harsh mechanical
clatter above his head. Suddenly the noise stopped. He
watched in horror as the now silent deadly machine
travelled over his head. It was losing height rapidly, and he
could see that it was heading straight down towards the
village school. As the grey flying bomb passed St Mary's
church Harry could hear the high-pitched laughter of the
children in the playground enjoying their morning break
time. ....

If you would like to go onto the email list to be advised the
moment part two becomes available, please go to
www.racingbooks.org

Maxwell Mark Power was born to the sound of screaming racing engines. His family lived just one mile from the Hanger Straight (as the crow flies) at Silverstone and it was British Grand Prix day.

Max grew up in a comfortable home with every spare space containing huge stacks of old Motor Sport and Autosport magazines and Motoring and Motorcycle Newspapers. Little wonder in his early years he thought motoring was the real world...the rest just strange.

His mother said his first word had been Mummy; in fact, it had been money.

Even at this young age, Max knew that if he wanted to be a racing driver he would need lots of money.

With single-minded determination, persistence and some skill Max did become a successful racing motorist firstly on motorbikes then with racing cars. Jetting off all over the world to the next race meeting but never staying anywhere long. When the scream of the last racing engine died away he would return home.

Max did enjoy win many races, but constant shortage of money and some HUGE crashes insured he never made the "big time".

A few times he has tried to retire from racing, but his addiction would always drag him back to the sport he loves. He now lives alone in his large workshop in the East of England surrounded by his trophies from old glories and bits of broken racing cars. However, he is still an optimist.

His motto " Where's the next race, I'm going to win this time"

13581166R00154

Printed in Germany
by Amazon Distribution
GmbH, Leipzig